The Magic Pony

Patricia Leitch started riding when a friend persuaded her to go on a pony trekking holiday – and by the following summer she had her own Highland pony, Kirsty. She wrote her first book shortly after this and writing is now her full-time occupation, but she has also done all sorts of different jobs, including being a riding-school instructor, groom, teacher and librarian. She lives in Renfrewshire, Scotland, with a bearded collie called Meg.

Patricia Leitch

The
Magic Pony

An Original Armada

The Magic Pony was first published in Armada in 1982
This impression 1988

Armada is an imprint of
the Children's Division, part of
the Collins Publishing Group,
8 Grafton Street, London W1X 3LA

Printed and bound in Great Britain by
William Collins Sons & Co. Ltd, Glasgow

CHAPTER ONE

"Who bloomin' cares?" thought Jinny Manders rebelliously. "Who cares what X equals? Not me. If I sat here forever I still couldn't find out," and she stared down at the algebra text-book open in front of her, hating its smug rows of meaningless equations. "What does it matter, anyway?"

It had been the mid-summer-term holiday. Riding home from school on Thursday, four days of freedom had stretched out before Jinny, four days when she could spend all her time with Shantih, her Arab mare; and now it was Monday evening, the long weekend wasted. Jinny's plans for a picnic ride to Loch Varrich and a day's ride to Miss Tuke's trekking centre had been washed out by three days of downpour. Three days of solid, pouring rain that had made any thoughts of riding an utter impossibility.

Jinny had tried to ride on Saturday morning, but after only twenty minutes she had been soaked to the skin, rain cascading from the brim of her hard hat, her newly-cleaned tack sodden and Shantih's red-gold coat sleeked to her body. Admitting defeat she had turned back home to Finmory House.

But Monday had been fine—blue sky with placid puffs of drifting white clouds.

"Think I'll ride to Miss Tuke's today," Jinny had told her family at breakfast. "Least the forestry tracks won't be flooded."

"You can't have forgotten?" said Petra, Jinny's elder sister.

"Forgotten what? What can't I have forgotten now?" demanded Jinny, glaring suspiciously at Petra, thinking how dreary it was to be thirteen and burdened with a sixteen-year-old sister who never forgot anything, never seemed to do anything wrong and, even at breakfast, looked crisp and bright.

"Go on, tell me, what have I forgotten?"

"We discussed it before I made the appointment," said her mother. "So there wouldn't be any fuss."

"Dentist," said Mike, Jinny's ten-year-old brother, pulling a face of agony.

And Jinny had remembered. The day had been arranged about a month ago. Dentist for them all first, then school shoes and new blazers.

"But I can't come," panicked Jinny. "Not when it's been so wet and I haven't been able to ride. It wouldn't be fair. You should have told me last night." But no one was paying any attention to her.

"Be ready for ten," Jinny's father said. He was driving them in to Inverburgh then going to see Nell Storr who had a gift shop in the town and sold the pottery that Mr. Manders and Ken Dawson, a boy who lived with them, made.

Dragging herself upstairs to get ready, Jinny abandoned all hope for the day. "But I'm riding tonight," she had promised herself. "I'm going for a gallop then. Nothing will stop me."

While the dentist was filling one of her back teeth, Jinny thought hard about galloping Shantih over the Finmory moors. She heard the thunder of Shantih's flying hoofbeats, felt her horse fit and eager, the wind blowing back the drift of Shantih's mane and her own long red hair as they galloped into the wind. All about them lay the open moorland and the glimmer of the sea in Finmory Bay.

"There we are," said the dentist. "Wasn't too bad, was it? Rinse out your mouth, please."

Jinny spat with enthusiasm, avoiding her hair. That was the worst part of the day over. Only buying clothes and back to Finmory. If they all got a move on they should be back for four at the latest, which left plenty of time for a long ride.

It was well after six before they got home. Mike's feet seemed to have reached an in-between stage not catered for by shoe manufacturers, and they had had to trail round dozens of shoe shops before they found a pair to fit him.

"At last!" Jinny had exclaimed as her father stopped the car outside Finmory House. "I'm going to ride *now*. At once. So don't anyone ask me to do anything."

"What about your algebra?" Petra had asked sweetly.

Half-way out of the car, Jinny froze with dismay. She had

8

completely forgotten about her algebra. On Thursday night, high on the thought of her four days holiday, she had made the mistake of pouring out her troubles to Petra, telling her how foul Mr. Palmer, her maths master, had been, saying that Jinny was lazy, insolent and totally inattentive. "And he gave me two punishment excercises to do for Tuesday," she had said. "Fourteen equations, all stupid letters instead of numbers. He knows I can't do them."

"Well, you'll need to, won't you?" Petra had said. "If it's a punishment exercise, you'll need to do it."

"What algebra?" her father demanded, turning round from the front of the car to look at Jinny. "Homework?"

"Oh, just some algebra I've to do," Jinny replied. "I'll do it when I come back from my ride."

"You'll do it before you ride," Mr. Manders had stated.

Jinny stared back at her father, wondering if it was worth arguing.

"Now," said Mr. Manders. "At once."

Into Jinny's mind swam the enraged face of Mr. Palmer when he had thrown her exercise book down on her desk and begun to tell her what he thought of her. He would not be happy if Jinny arrived at his class on Tuesday without having done the two exercises that he had given her.

"Blast!" exclaimed Jinny, which was the nearest her family allowed to swearing. "All weekend I haven't been able to ride and now it's fine I've to go and do bloomin' equations."

Jinny slammed the car door shut and stomped her way into the kitchen. Ken Dawson was baking bread. Kelly, his grey, shaggy dog lay stretched in a patch of sunlight. Ken was eighteen. He was tall and lanky with fair, shoulder-length hair. His rich parents sent him a cheque every month, but apart from that they had washed their hands of him. In the kitchen garden he had created at Finmory Ken grew all the fruit and vegetables that the Manders needed. He himself ate nothing that came from animals. "How can you say you love animals when you slaughter them for food? Kill days-old calves so you can drink the milk that was meant for them?"

"Hi," he said, looking up as Jinny burst in. "Had a happy family shopping trip?"

"Do I look it?" said Jinny, fending off Kelly's welcome. "Been to the dentist, had a filling, been dragged round every

9

shoe shop in Inverburgh and now, now when I was going to ride, I've to go and do algebra."

Jinny marched on out of the kitchen, up the broad flight of stairs, along the long corridor past bedroom and bathroom doors, until she came to the almost-vertical ladder of stairs that led up to her own bedroom. Crashing up the stairs, Jinny pushed open her door. She ran across her room, sprang on to her bed and stared out through the open window over Finmory's reach of garden, past the stables to their field where two horse shapes—dark against the green of the grass and the brightness of the sea dazzle—were grazing intently. One was Shantih, Jinny's chestnut Arab mare, the other was Bramble, a black Highland pony on loan from Miss Tuke's trekking centre.

"Shantih," Jinny called, leaning out of the window. "Shantih!"

The Arab lifted her head, ears pricked at the sound of Jinny's voice, her lustrous eyes wide as she looked around for her mistress.

"Shantih!"

Shantih whinnied with a tremble of sound and came, stepping delicately, precisely, towards the hedge closest to Finmory House. She stood at the hedge gazing up at Jinny, her nostrils still fluttering a greeting.

Next to her family and Ken, Shantih was the being closest to Jinny's heart. Two years ago Shantih had been in a circus, billed as Yasmin the Killer Horse. Now she belonged to Jinny. At first she had been wild and untamed and sometimes even Jinny had almost despaired of calming her. But now she had almost forgotten her fears of the ringmaster's whip, had stopped her frenetic rearing and mad runaways. Although she was still as fast as ever and could jump as if her heels carried wings, now she accepted Jinny's authority, shared gladly in the partnership of horse and rider.

"Dear horse," said Jinny lovingly, and with every atom of her being she longed to run into the open air and be riding Shantih over the moors.

With a great camel groan, Jinny turned away from the window. She went under the archway that divided her room into two and sat down at her table, dragged her algebra books from her schoolbag and stared despondently down at them.

The window in this half of Jinny's room looked out over the Finmory moors to the far blue mountains. The walls of the room were covered with Jinny's paintings and drawings, but on the wall facing her was a mural of a red horse.

When the Manders family had left the city suffocation of Stopton and come to live in the grey stone fastness of Finmory House, the Red Horse had been waiting for them. During the day, it was only a crude painting of a red horse with yellow eyes that plunged through a jungle of fleshy blue and green leaves and drooping white flowers, but by night there was a strange magic power belonging to the Horse. Jinny shuddered, goose over grave, remembering how last summer the Red Horse had haunted her dreams. She shrugged the memory away, determinedly opened her books and copied out the first equation.

Almost an hour later she was still staring down at the meaningless figures. Outside, the bright evening was beginning to fade. If she didn't get up and go now it would be too late to ride Shantih.

"If I stay here all night I'll never, ever, be able to do them." For minutes longer she sat wriggling on her chair, tipping it backwards and forwards as if trying to escape.

"I don't care," she said aloud. "I don't care what he says. Old potty Palmer! He can keep me in all week if he likes, but I'm going for a ride." And Jinny sprang from her chair and fled downstairs.

"Jinny," her father's voice shouted, as she passed the door of his pottery. "Have you finished your homework?"

"Done all I can," she yelled back, racing on.

In the kitchen, Petra was arranging her collections of pressed flowers.

"And how much was that?" she asked.

"No one," said Jinny, "was speaking to you."

"Bet you haven't done any."

"Wrong, as usual." And Jinny was out of the house before Petra could find out the truth.

"Whee!" she breathed, dropping to a slow loping trot. "Near thing."

Mrs. Manders jack-in-the-boxed from behind a row of raspberries.

"Remember," she said. "You must wash your hair."

"Glory hallelujah!" exclaimed Jinny. "I don't know why you can't all leave me alone. Nagging on at me."

"Jinny," warned her mother.

"But you do, you do. All the time."

"Are you going for a ride?"

"Yes, I am."

"Then come home past the farm and bring the milk," said Mrs. Manders. "And don't stay out too long."

"Don't stay out too long," said Jinny, managing to speak at exactly the same time as her mother. "Honestly, you'd think all I do is gallop over the moors at midnight."

"It has been known," said her mother, but Jinny was away.

She ran into the stables, grabbed Shantih's bridle and saddle and ran on down to the horses' field where Shantih was standing looking over the gate.

"Bet you're bored too. Stuck in that field for four days. Come on. We're going for a gallop."

As Jinny pushed the gate open, Shantih half reared, throwing up her neck, tossing her head, plunging away from Jinny into a sudden mad flurry of swirling mane and tail, a pounding drum-beat of hooves as she circled the field making Bramble gloom and glower. Then back at a full gallop to skid to a halt inches from Jinny.

"Idiot," said Jinny lovingly. "Bat brain."

Shantih lowered her head, accepting the bit and stood patiently while Jinny buckled on her bridle and saddled her. Jinny led Shantih out of the field and, gathering up her reins, sprang easily on to her back.

"The moor or the shore?" Jinny asked, gazing around her, hesitating. Then she knew. Between now and the moment when she climbed into the school bus, was marched into the prison of school, the moment when Mr. Palmer asked her for her algebra, she had to do everything, had to have such a ride on Shantih that all the boring miseries of tomorrow wouldn't matter. "Both," said Jinny. "Ride such a ride as never we rode before," and she turned Shantih towards Finmory Bay, letting her canter on with a long flowing stride.

They clattered over the bulwark of sea-smoothed boulders and the glimmering sands stretched before them. Jinny gave

Shantih her head. "On you go," she murmured, as Shantih bucked, stretched out her neck and was away.

In an ecstasy of speed, Jinny crouched low over her horse's neck. The screaming of the gulls and the brightness of the shore were all about her as they raced over the sands. She turned Shantih in a wide circle and galloped back until they came to a narrow track that climbed from the shore to the moors.

Shantih plunged upwards, digging her toes into the stony ground, humping suddenly forward as the rain-drenched earth gave way beneath her and cascades of stones made mini-avalanches down to the shore.

Over the moors they galloped. Dry-stone walls rose up before them and fell away behind them as Shantih soared over them and galloped on. There was no tomorrow, only this now of space and light. Joy in Shantih and in this flying freedom sang through Jinny's whole being. She rode entranced, the Arab mare part of her own being. On and on they went.

Then, against the skyline, Jinny saw the black fingers of the standing stones. She was back in Time. She slowed Shantih to a trot and then to a walk. Conscious now of the grey evening, Jinny knew that she had come too far. It would certainly be what her mother considered late before Jinny reached home. She turned Shantih round and began to ride back. Shantih crabbed, half rearing, wanting to gallop on.

"No way," Jinny told her, sitting down firmly, forcing her on. "We have had it. They will all be furious. We've got to get back."

They were in sight of Finmory when Jinny remembered about the milk. "Mr. MacKenzie will be in bed by now,' she thought, and wondered if her family really needed the milk, if there would be lost tempers if she didn't get it.

"Honestly," she told Shantih, as they rode down towards Finmory. "All my life is nothing but other people bossing me around. I hate them all. Why can't they leave me alone? Leave me alone to do the things I want to do. All I want is to be left alone to ride and draw, but oh no, Jinny do this, Jinny do that. Teachers shouting at me, all week shut up in that prison of a school, and then, when I do get home, I've to spend all my time running errands."

Jinny stared out balefully over the darkening moors. Black clouds lying low over the sea had turned it into dark mercury. The rocks at either side of the bay were ebony jaws poised to kill. The coming night reached long shadowy fingers over the rough moorland. Shantih's hoofs dipped into pools of shadow. And tomorrow Mr. Palmer waited for the alegbra that Jinny hadn't done. Another detention meant a visit to the Headmaster.

Suddenly Jinny gathered up her reins and urged Shantih on into a gallop. The stone wall dividing Finmory's land from the moors stretched in front of them. Normally Jinny would have ridden through the open gateway, but tonight, her black mood heavy upon her, she rode Shantih straight at the wall.

Shantih pounded up to it, and Jinny saw that it was higher than she had realised. In daylight she would never have dreamed of jumping it. As Shantih rose to clear it, Jinny knotted her fingers into Shantih's mane, saw Shantih's neck arched, her ears pricked, caught a glimpse of her forelegs tucked close into her body. Suddenly, from the other side of the wall, a sheep erupted into life. In mid-air, Shantih screwed herself sideways, eyes bulging with terror. She landed awkwardly, fought to stay on her feet, then fell. Jinny saw the ground coming up to knock the breath out of her. She lay plastered flat against it, watching helplessly as Shantih struggled to rise.

It was minutes before Jinny managed to get up and stagger across to where Shantih stood, her head almost touching the ground, blood trickling down her shoulder.

"Shantih!" cried Jinny, appalled at what she had done. "Oh Shantih! There, the horse." She rubbed the sleeve of her anorak over the cut in Shantih's shoulder and saw, to her relief, that it was little more than a scratch. Urgently, Jinny looked at Shantih's knees and legs and ran her hands over her quarters searching for any other cuts, but as far as Jinny could see in the half-dark, Shantih was unhurt.

Jinny collapsed on the ground.

"Jinny Manders, you fool, you lunatic. How could you be so stupid," she told herself.

Looking up at the wall, Jinny saw that where she had jumped it there had been an enormous drop on the landing side. Even without the sheep hazard it would have been a risky landing.

Jinny shuddered, stood up, and still shaken by her fall, didn't remount but took Shantih's reins and began to lead her downhill. Coming down in the gathering dark, Shantih seemed unsure of her footing, stumbling and tripping over loose stones and heather roots. Even when they reached the track that led to Mr. MacKenzie's farm, Shantih still seemed to be stumbling far more than usual. Twice, Jinny, plodding on ahead of her horse, nearly had the reins pulled out of her hands as Shantih lost her balance.

Mr. MacKenzie opened the farmhouse door as he heard them approach. He stood in the shaft of golden electric light that suddenly made the dim grey evening change into darkness, and watched them coming into his yard.

"I've come for the milk," Jinny said, trying to make her voice sound easy, as if it was the afternoon, wondering how late it really was.

"Would that be so?" said Mr. MacKenzie, reaching up for his cap, putting it on the back of his head and pulling it well down over his gimlet eyes. "I'm thinking it's the blessing you're not for the duck eggs, or the wee bit ducklings would have been swimming away by this time," and the old man led the way across the yard to the byre.

"It's the roll in the mud you've been having to yourselves," he said, as he picked up the full milk can and handed it to Jinny. "Haven't I been warning you until I'm sick of the sound of my own voice, not to be riding over those hills in the dark?"

"Not you too," said Jinny in disgust. "It wasn't dark when we set out."

"Is that a fact? Well, it's the dark now, I'm thinking, and from the sound of your horse's feet it's herself will be lame tomorrow."

"What do you mean? Shantih's not lame."

"And why would you be leading her? Away home with you and be listening to her ladyship as you go."

The door of the farmhouse snicked shut behind the farmer as Jinny screwed up her face at his departing back.

"What does he know?" she said to Shantih. "Always minding other people's business. You're not lame, are you? You're

O.K. Of course you're not lame." Jinny ran her hand down Shantih's sleek neck, pulled her ear through her hand as Shantih pitched forward, stumbling so badly that her muzzle touched the ground.

When Jinny had listened to her parents' angry anxiety she went upstairs and washed her hair. While she was drying it she heard her family going to bed, the house sinking into silence. She was just going to get undressed when she changed her mind, pulled on her anorak and crept downstairs. She took her father's powerful torch from the kitchen dresser and eased the key round in the back door. The golden circle of torchlight slid in front of her as she made her way down to the horses' field.

"Shantih," Jinny called, as she climbed over the gate. "Come on then, Shantih."

She swung the swathe of torchlight over the field, picked out the bulk of Bramble lying at the hedge roots, then Shantih standing close by.

"Shantih," Jinny called again, and the Arab began to walk slowly towards her, her stride uneven, plucking up her left foreleg almost before it touched the ground. Before Jinny had left her she had picked out her hooves, checked her legs for any cuts or scratches but had found none.

As the Arab came closer, Jinny saw her head nod forward with the tight, almost imperceptible grimace of pain. There was no doubt about it, Mr. MacKenzie had been right, Shantih was lame.

"And I did it," Jinny thought. "It's all my fault for making her jump that wall."

CHAPTER TWO

The next morning, Shantih was still lame. Mr. Manders had to drive Jinny into Glenbost, the nearest crofting village to Finmory. Normally Jinny rode Shantih into Glenbost and left her in a field while she caught the school bus to the comprehensive school in Inverburgh. Mike, who went to the Glenbost primary school, rode Bramble, leaving her in the field with Shantih. Petra, who was a weekly boarder at Duninver High School, was collected on Monday mornings by a school taxi.

"Come on, Jinny. Hurry up!" said Mr. Manders irritably, as he waited, still gritty with sleep, for his daughter to organise herself into the car.

"I have to be out every morning at this time," Jinny told him, climbing in beside her father and slamming the car door.

" 'The hoar necessitous horror of the morning'," quoted Mr. Manders.

"Will you phone the vet?" asked Jinny urgently.

"Don't panic. Couldn't we leave her for a day or two? Might only be a twist. It might get better by itself."

"No. Of course not. She's really lame. Say it was something that needed treatment right away and we didn't get the vet. Then when he came he said she'd never be sound again because we hadn't called him in earlier? How would we feel then?"

"Or, of course, she may have dropped dead in the field by now so there's no point in worrying."

"It's not funny," said Jinny. "Not anything to make jokes about."

"Sorry," said Mr. Manders. "Blame the hour. I'll phone when I get back. Better if he comes tonight when you're there to hear what he has to say." He slowed the car to a crawl as Mr. MacKenzie and two sheepdogs came towards them, a froth of sheep filling the road.

"Aye," Mr. MacKenzie greeted them. "A fine morning."

17

"Grand," agreed Mr. Manders impatiently, as the farmer stopped and leant an elbow on the open window of the car.

"It's yourself has the chauffeur this morning?" he said to Jinny. "And it's surprised I am that you're even fit to be driven to the school after your madness on the hill last night."

Jinny scowled up at him.

"What madness?" demanded Mr. Manders.

"Sailing over walls that would have stopped Red Rum himself. And I'm thinking from the mess of the good ground, it's the wee tumble you had to yourselves. She'll be lame this morning, I'm thinking."

"Oh yes," said Jinny. "You're thinking right as usual. Shantih's lame. And if we don't get a move on, I'm going to miss the bus."

"No foot, no hoss," said Mr. MacKenzie, savouring the thought. "No foot, no hoss."

"And what was all that about?" asked Mr. Manders as they drove away.

Reluctantly, Jinny told her father about last night's fall. "Though how Mr. MacKenzie found out about it, I don't know. Must have been up at dawn searching the moors for hoofprints."

"Honestly Jinny, at times I utterly despair of you. What makes you do such stupid things?"

"The bus," cried Jinny, catching a glimpse of familiar red bus on the road from Ardtallon. "Oh quick, hurry up. Dougal won't wait for me if I'm not there."

Mr. Manders put his foot down and they reached Glenbost at the same time as the bus.

"We'll meet you," he called. "If there's no one there, start walking."

"Be sure to phone the vet," Jinny reminded him, as she scrambled out of the car and ran towards the bus.

"Lucky you are that you weren't late this morning," Dolina Thompson said, squashing up on her seat to make room for Jinny beside her. Dolina had gone to Glenbost School and was in the same class as her at Inverburgh. "It's the black dog Dougal has sitting on his shoulder this morning."

"Not the only one," said Jinny, flopping down beside her.

"Aye," said Dolina, turning flat cod eyes to survey Jinny's

18

turned-up collar and uncombed hair. "It's the look of the jumble you have on you yourself."

"Shantih's lame," said Jinny, and told Dolina what had happened.

"Och, I wouldn't be worrying yourself about that. When we'd the old pony for the ploughing, he was lame all the time, but a wee bit work soon took his mind off it."

"Honestly!" exclaimed Jinny. "Fancy working a lame pony."

"What's more to the point," said Dolina. "Have you done the algebra for Mr. Palmer? I'm thinking he'll be having the wee turn if you haven't it finished for him."

"Well, I haven't," said Jinny. "So he'll just need to have a wee turn. I can't help it. Bad enough Shantih being lame without worrying over stupid things like algebra."

"You know the maps we've to do for the geography? Well, I was just thinking I could be doing the algebra for you and you could be copying it out before we reach the school, and maybe you could be drawing the map for me before Thursday? It's the wee arrangement we could have?"

Jinny hesitated. She knew what her parents would think about Dolina's wee arrangement, but it would save so much trouble. Save all that shouting when Mr. Palmer discovered that Jinny hadn't done the wretched algebra.

"Oh, O.K." agreed Jinny, opening her schoolbag. "Need to be quick. He gave me two excercises to do."

As if they had been simple additions, Dolina worked her way through the equations and Jinny copied them down into her exercise book.

"It's the kindness we're doing him," said Dolina smugly. "You can see to look at him that he has the raging blood pressure. It'll be much easier this way."

"Dolina was right," Jinny thought at the end of the algebra lesson when Mr. Palmer had taken her excercise book, glanced at it to make sure that she had done the work, grunted and put it on top of the pile of books on his desk.

Jim Rae, the vet, came that evening, listened to Jinny's explanation of Shantih's fall, then told Jinny to trot Shantih up and down keeping the halter rope loose. As Jinny ran at Shantih's head she felt the uneven beat of Shantih's stride.

"She's worse," Jinny thought, as several times Shantih

stumbled, nearly coming down on her knees as she tried to avoid putting any weight on the left foreleg.

"She's lame, O.K." said the vet. "Near fore. No doubt about that. Poor woman. Now, let's see if we can find out what's causing it."

Jinny stood holding Shantih as the vet ran his hand down Shantih's leg, his strong, sensitive fingers searching for unusual lumps or swellings. He picked up Shantih's hoof, examined it thoroughly, felt the wall of the hoof for heat and tapped it with a small hammer, but Shantih showed no reaction. She stood staring out over Jinny's shoulder, apparently feeling no pain.

At last the vet straightened up.

"Can't see a thing," he said. "She doesn't seem to feel anything in her foot. No heat, no swelling in her leg. Nothing showing. Could be her shoulder, but from the way she was moving I'd swear it's her leg or foot. Just need to wait and see."

"You mean you can't do anything for her," demanded Jinny aghast.

"Could be a sprain, a twist. Leave her out and don't ride her until the weekend. If she's still lame, give me a phone and I'll come out and take another look at her. Meanwhile I'll give her a shot in case there's any poison in her. She's had an anti-tet., hasn't she?"

"Yes," said Jinny, watching the sure, automatic movements of the vet's hands as he injected Shantih.

"That's the woman," he said, clapping Shantih on the neck, turning to go. "Dare say she'll sort herself out in a day or two."

But Shantih didn't. A week later she was still as lame as ever. The vet had been back but couldn't find any reason for the lameness. There was no heat, no swelling, but Shantih was dead lame. Jinny spent her time leaning over the field gate watching her horse limping about.

"Even a slightly twisted ankle can take weeks to stop hurting," he mother reassured her. "Give her time."

But Jinny's heart was heavy with guilt. She knew that if she hadn't jumped that wall Shantih wouldn't be dragging round the field, the light and fire gone from her.

Jinny had phoned Miss Tuke to see if she could give her

any help, but Miss Tuke was too busy organising her trek-kers to have any time for Jinny.

"Told you before you'd break that mare's leg galloping her about the way you do. If Jim Rae can't find out what the trouble is, there's no point in me coming over. Hock-deep in trekkers. Haven't a sec. to spare."

"Thank you very much, Miss Tuke," said Jinny, when she had put the phone down.

The blacksmith, who always came on to Finmory after he had shod Miss Tuke's trekkers, had taken the shoe off Shan-tih's near fore. But he too had shaken his head.

"I wouldn't be saying it's the shoe, though if the vet wants it off, off it will come. There's not a thing I can see wrong with the poor brute's leg. Probably a twist, though she's feeling it, a blind man could see that."

"There must be someone else who knows about horses," Jinny complained to Ken. "Must be."

"Heard about someone who treated animals with homoeo-pathic medicine," said Ken.

"Where?" said Jinny, clutching at straws, not even too sure what homoeopathic medicine was.

"Amsterdam," said Ken.

"A-plus for useless, pointless information," said Jinny, swinging away from him.

It wasn't until the next Wednesday afternoon that Jinny heard about someone who might be able to help. Dolina had persuaded Jinny to help with the tea for a choir from St. Margaret's, private girls' school in Inverburgh, who were giving a performance at the comprehensive school on Wednesday.

"We'll miss double science," coaxed Dolina, and Jinny had agreed to volunteer.

She was standing behind the long table making sure there were enough cups and saucers, filling up the milk jugs and sugar bowls, when one of the St. Margaret's girls spoke to her.

"You must be Jinny Manders?" the girl said.

"Yes," said Jinny, looking suspiciously at the tall, dark-haired girl who had spoken to her.

"The one who has an Arab and rides it to school?"

"Well, into Glenbost and then bus, but not at all just now. She's lame."

21

"Oh, that's a pity," said the girl. "I'm Joyce West. My aunt is friends with one of your staff. And when she heard about you she told me, seeing I'm horse-daft. Sorry to hear your Arab's lame. What's wrong?"

"Don't know," said Jinny, welcoming a sympathetic ear. "Even the vet doesn't seem to know. She's been lame for nearly two weeks now and she's not getting any better. The vet just keeps on saying it's a twist and to give it time."

"Front leg?"

"Yes. Near fore."

"How maddening. Especially when there's nothing you can do."

"I know. And she isn't getting any better. It's dreadful not being able to ride her and utterly dreadful watching her limping round the field and not being able to do anything to help her."

"Do you know what could have caused it?"

"She came down after we'd jumped a wall," Jinny muttered, feeling her stomach clench cold and tight with guilt.

"Could easily have sprained it," comforted Joyce. "Or it might be a puncture. Could it be a nail? I knew a horse who was bedded on woodshavings. There was a nail left in them and she got it right into her foot. It took the vet weeks to find out what was wrong. No sign at all from the outside."

"Shantih hasn't been near any nails so I don't think it could be that," said Jinny. "If only I knew someone really horsy who could come and look at her for me." Jinny looked hopefully at Joyce.

"Not me. Sorry. Horse-daft but I'm no expert. I just ride at a riding school."

"Near here?" asked Jinny.

"Not far. About three-quarters of an hour's walk. Bit grotty, but we get quite a good canter along the edge of a golf course."

"Is there anyone there who might come and look at Shantih?"

"Brenda Digby. She runs the riding school. Been around horses all her life. She might, if you asked her. Look, why don't you come for a ride? I ride on the eleven o'clock ride on a Saturday morning. Come then."

"This Saturday," said Jinny eagerly.

"Oh no. No use. I'll not be there. How about the next? Or go yourself. Listen, I've to phone up to cancel. Shall I tell Brenda you'll take my place?"

"Right," said Jinny, suddenly seeing Brenda as a tall, elegant horsewoman who would gladly come out to Finmory and, after years of horsy experience, know instantly how to cure Shantih's lameness.

"It's called the Arran Riding School. Here, I'll draw you a map of how to get there." Taking a pen from her blazer pocket, Joyce drew a quick sketch-map on a paper napkin of how to reach the riding school from Inverburgh bus station.

"Could I have some money, please?" Jinny asked her father. "I'm going for a ride at a riding school on Saturday morning."

"Riding school?" said Mr. Manders. "What on earth for? You can ride Bramble, can't you?"

"I met this girl who told me about it. The woman who runs it has worked with horses all her life, so I thought if I went for a ride I could get to know her and I could ask her about Shantih."

"But surely she won't know more than the vet?"

"She might," said Jinny. "Jim Rae doesn't see all that many horses. All sheep and cows he deals with."

In Jinny's mind was a clear picture of Brenda Digby. After her career with horses she was bound to know more than the vet. Probably she had worked with hunters and show ponies; even possible that she had worked in racing stables. Jinny saw her with short wavy hair, dressed in an elegantly-cut hacking jacket and cord slacks, striding across the field to Shantih, picking up Shantih's leg and saying, "Nothing to worry about here. I'll tell you what to do. Have her sound in no time."

"Rather a long shot," said Mr. Manders dubiously. "Isn't the vet coming on Saturday?"

"No. Friday night. So please may I have some money?"

Rather reluctantly, Mr. Manders handed over five pounds. "There had better be change," he said.

"Bound to be. Thanks." said Jinny, pocketing the note quickly before he changed his mind.

Jinny rode Bramble into Glenbost early on Saturday morning.

"I know it's not a work day," she said, kicking on the stubborn pony. "But just for once you are going to have to work overtime and lump it."

Bramble pinned back his ears and switched his tail.

"Be thankful," Jinny told him, "that you're not Shantih." Sitting down hard in the saddle, she forced him into an unwilling trot.

"Still no improvement," the vet had said the night before. "Can be the dickens to find out what's wrong when it's their feet. I'll pop back at the beginning of the week and give her an injection that will stop all feeling in her foot. If she goes sound after that, we'll know it *is* her foot."

"And once we know it is her foot," thought Jinny, kicking Bramble harder than ever, "What then? What's he going to do then to cure her?"

Jinny caught the Inverburgh bus by the skin of her teeth. Trying to follow Joyce's map, she took a wrong turning and took ages finding her way back.

"Going to be late," she thought, as she raced along the road to the stables. "Not going to have time to talk to Brenda before the ride."

Now that she was nearly there, Jinny's stomach was beginning to turn over. She had only been to one other riding school in her life. That had been Major Young's place in Stopton. It had been very superior, with an immaculate yard, well-groomed horses and equally well-groomed riders. But as Jinny turned down a lane by the side of a golf course and saw a huddle of ramshackle buildings in front of her and a weather-faded riding-school sign nailed to a tree, she realised that the Arran Riding School wasn't going to be at all like Major Young's. Half of Jinny was relieved that it wasn't going to be a posh place, but half was already beginning to realise that if Brenda worked in a place like this she wasn't likely to be much help with Shantih.

Jinny went through a gateway, gingerly opening and shutting a gate that threatened to fall to pieces when it was touched. On her left was a small cottage, its paint peeling, its walls stained green where rain had poured down from the broken guttering, its small windowpanes grimy with dirt. Over the porch at the front door, rambler roses swarmed in unpruned confusion.

Jinny walked along the hedge that encircled the wilderness cottage garden, following it round to a small field where several jumps were set up in the middle of a rutted schooling circle. At the field gate, oil drums and broken poles were piled in high battlements but there was no sign of any life.

Jinny hesitated, listening. Then, hearing the sound of voices, she retraced her steps and followed a muddy track through a narrow opening between two outhouses that seemed to be made of old doors and sheets of corrugated iron. She came out into a stable yard.

Along one side of the yard were four looseboxes in the same state of disrepair as the rest of the buildings. On the opposite side was a long, low building and, through its open door, Jinny glimpsed a row of narrow stalls. More rusted oil drums were piled in a corner of the yard, a water trough was half-filled with stagnant water, and heaps of dung were swept into corners.

Jinny saw these things but hardly noticed them. She had eyes for nothing but the ponies and horses. There were two bay fifteen-hand horses—one that looked almost a thorough-bred. Its coat was sparse and staring, stretched tight over ribs and gaunt hip bones. Its neck was so thin that Jinny could clearly see the ridging of its larynx. Its hocks and elbows were capped and its knees badly scarred from an old fall. Its tail hung down in a fouled wisp of hair and its quarters were deeply grooved with poverty lines. The other looked as if it had been put together from parts of several different horses—its heavy head too large for its long neck, its slab-sided body supported by four misshapen legs—legs which were lumped and bumped with splints and spavins and old scars.

Of the four ponies, one was a heavy Highland, its shrunken body still covered in patches of winter coat, its blubbery lower lip hanging open almost touching the ground as it stood with its head drooping lifelessly. One was a 12.2 dark brown pony with fine-boned legs and a world-weary face. Its long feet were turning up with laminitis. One was a fourteen-hand chestnut; its fiddle-face on an upside-down neck was strapped in with a tight standing martingale attached to a drop noseband. The fourth pony was a black 14.2 with a white face. It had an open girth gall, rubbed raw by an iron-hard, leather girth.

All the tack was dried and cracked. Some of the ponies were unshod, with cracked, breaking hooves, while others had thin, smooth-worn shoes, the risen clinches sticking up from their hooves.

Jinny felt sick. She couldn't believe it possible, couldn't believe that anyone could work horses like these. They were worse than the ponies that had pulled carts in Stopton, worse than the blackest of Jinny's imaginings. She stood staring, the scream that was always inside her when she really thought how cruelly people treated animals, tightening her throat, crushing her skull. Yet the girls holding the ponies were smiling, chatting, excited at the thought of going for a ride.

"Hi!" called the girl holding the two horses. "You must be Jinny. I'm Moira. Joyce told me you were coming. Think you're to ride Sporty." She gestured towards the jig-saw horse. "I'm riding Queenie. Those two always stick together so you'll be O.K. Better wait until Brenda comes out before you get on."

Jinny hardly heard her. She wanted to turn and run from the horrors of the place, but she stood unable to move.

A girl in smart riding clothes came along the path behind Jinny. For a second Jinny thought this must be Brenda, then saw that she was too young.

"Hi!" Moira shouted to the smart girl. "You've to ride Easter. Brenda said to get her out when you arrived."

The girl smiled a thin-lipped, nervous smile and, crossing the yard, went into the row of stalls. She came out leading an aged white pony of fourteen hands. She was poor, as all the others were poor, with ridged ribs, sunken quarters and scarred legs. Her dark eyes, fringed with black lashes and long, straying hairs, were lustrous in her skeletal head. Her mane was a tangle of witch-knots and her long tail twisted into cords of hair. All the others were old, but this pony was like a ghost—so old she seemed hardly there, unable to stand against the assault of the light.

The scream tore out of Jinny in a sudden gasp of sound. For the spirit that was almost visible in the white pony was that of a top-class show pony, fleet and beautiful beyond the singing of it.

"What's up?" demanded Moira. "Are you feeling sick? You've gone dead white."

Jinny stammered for words to shield her, and Brenda came out from one of the sheds.

"Everyone ready?" she asked. "Get up then."

Brenda was small and dumpy. Faded jeans stretched over a broad bottom, short fat legs squashed into wellingtons, a dirty blue anorak strained at its fastenings. Her hair was dyed red with henna, her face was pink with make-up, orange lipstick spread over her lips.

"You the girl instead of Joyce?" she asked Jinny, a cigarette bobbing in the corner of her mouth.

Dumbly, Jinny nodded.

"Ride Sporty. Moira will keep an eye on you."

As if in a trance, Jinny took Sporty's reins, tightened his girth, pulled down the rusty stirrups and mounted.

Riding a bay horse with a Roman nose, Brenda led the way out of the yard. The horses, as if they were programmed automata, turned and followed her.

They rode along the track at the side of the golf course in a slow straggle, except for the girl on the chestnut, who had quickly been carted past Brenda and was struggling to hold back her pony as it fought, half rearing, to break away from her control.

"Are you O.K.?" Moira asked. riding at Jinny's side. "You'll need to kick him on a bit. Get him going. Good job we're not in the paddock. He'd just stand still with you there. What you need is a stick. Pity we didn't think of it before. There's plenty old ones lying about the tack room."

Jinny closed her ears to Moira's chatter. She had never ridden anything like Sporty before. His sides were completely dead, without feeling, and his lips so calloused that he hardly seemed to notice the bit in his mouth. Jinny ran her hand down his scrawny neck, making much of him, talking gently to him, but he plodded woodenly on, giving no sign that he knew Jinny was riding him.

When they reached the end of the track, the ride turned round and headed back to the stables. They reached the stables, turned, and rode back alongside the golf course.

"Do you always just ride up and down here?" Jinny asked.

"No. 'Course not. Sometimes we go for road rides or in the paddock. Are you getting bored? Well, you needn't be. Next time back, we trot and then we canter.

27

Jinny wanted to say, "Big deal," but she bit the words back as she longed desperately for the ride to be over so that she would no longer be part of the dismal procession.

When they trotted back, the chestnut pony took off at a mad tearaway gallop.

"Always does that," confided Moira. "Brenda gets furious. Says we can't ride or we could stop him. Still, doesn't matter, he always does stop at the stables."

Sporty's trot threw Jinny up and down in the saddle. Each leg seemed to be doing its own thing as he battered along. When at last they cantered, Jinny, used to Shantih's smooth paces, was tossed about in the saddle like a cork on a rough sea.

"You haven't ridden much, have you?" stated Moira. "Bet you're not bored now."

Jinny thought of telling her about Shantih, but changed her mind. There was no point. Moira wouldn't have believed her.

Once, Jinny glanced back and glimpsed Easter, the white pony, moving with a showy, toe-pointing stride. Her thin neck was arched and her head tucked in, a pathetic echo of her past. Quickly, Jinny looked round again, tears stinging behind her eyes, a lump hard in her throat.

"Any use?" asked Mr. Manders, when at last Jinny was home again.

"The end," said Jinny, giving him back two pounds. "Terrible, terrible place. The horses were awful—worn out, ancient. They should all have been retired years ago. There was one white pony—I'm sure she must have been a show pony once, years ago. But now . . ."

Words failed Jinny, but Ken nodded, understanding, sharing her heartbreak and useless fury. Out of all the people Jinny knew, Ken was the only one who really cared about animals. Not as pets or show objects or for their speed or usefulness to humans. He cared that they should be free to be themselves. Ken was the one person who would really understand how Jinny felt about the white pony.

"They shouldn't be allowed to run a place like that," said Jinny. " The R.S.P.C.A. should close it down."

"Can't you do something about it?" asked Mr. Manders. "If it's as bad as you say it is, I'm sure something could be done about it."

"I'll ask the vet," said Jinny, "the next time he's here. He's bound to know it."

Jinny went out and down to Shantih, the blackness of the riding school still filling her mind. She gave Shantih an apple and ran her hand down her horse's firm neck, over her withers, and stretched her arm over her broad strong back. She straightened the fine hair of Shantih's forelock so that it lay in a silken tassel along her white face.

"You will never become like them," she promised, as Shantih lipped at her hand hoping for more titbits. "When you're old you'll have the moors and a warm stable when you want it."

Then into Jinny's head came Mr. MacKenzie's voice. "No foot, no hoss," it said. "No foot, no hoss."

CHAPTER THREE

It was the Thursday after Jinny's visit to the riding school and Jinny was sitting at the back of Mr. Palmer's algebra class. Presumably Mr. Palmer was standing at the front teaching algebra. Jinny wasn't listening. She was thinking about Shantih and drawing a picture of herself jumping Shantih over a stone wall. Jinny had got into so much trouble over drawing in her school exercise books that now she carried a drawing pad with her and drew on that. With an exact, precise line, Jinny's pencil moved over the blank page and Shantih, full of grace and joy, came to life. Jinny found it easier to think while she was drawing.

The vet had injected Shantih's leg on Sunday morning and by the afternoon she was going sound, proving that the lameness was in her foot. He had told Jinny to try hosing Shantih's foot with cold water, so in the mornings before school and in the evenings after school Jinny was hosing Shantih's leg, but with no result. The vet was coming back on Saturday morning.

"He just doesn't know what to do," Jinny thought miserably. "He doesn't know any more than I do and all this time Shantih's suffering. He doesn't really care either, not the way I do . . ."

"Jinny," hissed the boy sitting next to her. "Wake up."

Jinny started back to the reality of the classroom, automatically covering her drawing with her algebra book.

"Now that you've condescended to give me your attention, for the third time of asking, will you come out to my desk?"

Watched by the rest of the class, Jinny made her way uncertainly to Mr. Palmer's desk. She couldn't think what he wanted. The punishment exercises she had copied from Dolina had come back to her with all the equations ticked correct and "is light beginning to dawn?" written at the foot of them. Jinny had spent nearly two hours struggling through the six equations that had been Monday's homework and, although she didn't think they would be correct,

30

she had got them all finished and handed them in on time.

"Now, Jinny," said Mr. Palmer, looking up from Jinny's algebra exercise book which was open in front of him. "Perhaps you can explain something for me. Here are the punishment exercises you did for me. All correct. And here is Monday's homework. Every one wrong, showing not even a basic understanding of equations. What happened between one exercise and the other? Eh?"

Staring, mesmerised by Mr. Palmer's bulging blue eyes, Jinny struggled to find an explanation.

"The first lot just seemed easier," she muttered lamely. "I could do them."

"Or somebody else could do them? Eh? Isn't that nearer the fact?"

Jinny felt herself blush scarlet—the whole class was listening. She could feel their staring prickling her spine. Memories of her primary school, when, without meaning to, she had got Dolina into trouble, swam back into Jinny's mind.

"Ken helped me," Jinny blurted out, changing her story in mid-stream. "He's a boy that lives with us."

"So you didn't find them easy? You needed help? Take a look at this."

A nicotine-stained forefinger directed Jinny's attention to one of the equations. At first it was only a jumble of meaningless letters and figures, and then Jinny saw what was wrong. Somehow in the workings she must have jumped from one equation to the next, then copied the correct answer.

"It's that rickety old school bus," Jinny thought. "Jumping about."

"I don't think anyone helped you. I think you copied them. I think someone in this class did them for you and you copied them down?"

Jinny paused to test the soundness of her lie, then, looking Mr. Palmer straight in the eye, said: "Ken did them. I copied them after he'd done them for me."

"I do not believe you," stated Mr. Palmer, "but I don't intend to waste any more time over you. You'll go to detention tonight and do the first of the punishment exercises then bring it to me in my room."

"Not detention. I can't. Mum or Dad meet me at Glenbost

because Shantih's lame. They'd be mad if I wasn't on the school bus."

"Give me your phone number and I'll let your parents know that you're being detained. Though, from the look of the detention book, I should think they must be quite used to your non-arrivals."

"Oh, you can't. There's no one at home today," said Jinny, panicked into instant lies by the thought of her maths teacher actually speaking to her father.

Without words, Mr. Palmer's look conveyed that once again he did not believe Jinny.

"Very well," he said. "Tell your parents that you will be in detention tomorrow. Now sit down and have the good manners to pay attention while I am teaching you."

As Jinny went back to her seat, Mr. Palmer's gaze picked out Dolina's bright pink face.

"Whoever did the equations for Jinny to copy was not doing her a favour. She is here to learn how to do algebra, not to learn how to cheat."

"Now Jinny, read out the next equation and we'll work it on the blackboard."

The girl in front of Jinny turned round and pointed out the equation. Jinny stood up and read it out.

"You could teach monkeys to read," she thought as she sat down. "You don't need to understand what you're reading to be able to read it." Then she thought "Shantih". Who would hose her foot on Friday evening and was it doing any good anyway? Jinny's eyes filled with sudden, infuriating tears.

The detention hour was almost over on Friday afternoon and Jinny was still struggling with the third equation, when Mr. Palmer came to the door of the detention room and beckoned her out.

"Right," he said. "Come along to my room and we'll go over them together."

Following Mr. Palmer down the corridor, Jinny glanced at her watch. It was five to five. If she missed the six o'clock bus there wasn't another one until eight o'clock. "Please don't let him keep me too long," she prayed. "Let me catch the six o'clock bus."

"I think," said Mr. Palmer, when he had looked at Jinny's

attempts to work out the equations, "we had better go back to basics."

Jinny groaned aloud.

Going back to basics took until a quarter to six. Dragging on her anorak, Jinny ran full pelt out of the school, across the yard and raced for the bus station. She was just in time to see her bus drawing away.

"Stop!" Jinny yelled. "Wait for me!" But the driver paid no attention to her.

"Doom and double doom," swore Jinny in a fury of utter frustration. "Oh curses, curses, curses. Two hours to wait when I should be at home hosing Shantih's leg. Bloomin' algebra. Bloomin' school. Blast it all."

For minutes Jinny stood fuming, but there was nothing she could do about it. The bus had gone and that was that. Slowly she wove her way through the people pouring into the bus station.

"All going home," thought Jinny, "and here I am stuck here for two hours."

She was going into a shop to buy a bar of chocolate when suddenly she changed her mind and went into the fruiterers next door.

"I'll buy two apples," she decided, "and take them to the white pony."

Now that Jinny had thought of something to do, the two hours she had to wait didn't seem nearly so long. She bought the apples and began to walk briskly out to the riding school, thoughts of Easter filling her head.

"If only they could talk," Jinny thought. "If only they could tell us what has happened to them. When she was a show pony what went wrong?" And Jinny imagined all the different things that could have happened to the white pony to bring her down in the world. Bought by rich parents for a daughter who was scared of her, then sold on as a dangerous runaway? Or kept until she was too old to win in the ring then sent to a sale? Or maybe when she was young she had been difficult to ride; perhaps only one girl could show her, and when the girl had to go abroad with her family the pony had reared in the show ring coming down on top of her rider, injuring her for life. Perhaps the pony had been sold cheaply to get rid of her.

Jinny had nearly reached the riding school when the sound of hooves made her stop and listen. Then, coming down the road towards her, was a ride being led by Brenda on her bay.

Jinny's heart sank with disappointment. Now she wouldn't be able to give the apples to Easter, for she could see the white pony trailing along behind the ride. The chestnut pony behind Brenda was already frothing at the mouth as the girl riding him tried to hold him back. Of all the horses, the chestnut was the only one who showed any life. The others walked slowly along, heads down, eyes half-closed, the clink of loose shoes ringing against the road as the ride dragged its way past Jinny.

Easter was being ridden by a heavy man sitting far back in the saddle, his legs stuck out in front, his elbows wide. In one hand he held the reins in a muddled twist of leather. In the other he held a long cutting whip.

"Get on, you lazy cow," the man shouted, kicking his feet against Easter's shoulders as he saw Jinny watching him.

The gaunt weariness of the white pony never changed. As if she moved through a nightmare, she walked on with a slow stride. Her harsh coat stretched tightly over her protruding bones as she moved.

The man jangled the rusty bit in Easter's mouth. "Gee up. Get on," he said, and hit the pony with his whip.

The white pony shuddered through her whole frame. For a second she seemed about to break into a trot. Almost, her head lifted, her eyes brightened and her worn-out limbs carried her sweetly, lightly, into an effortless trot. Almost, but not quite. Before she actually changed from her slow, dragging walk, she fell back into the reality of her age, the reality of what it meant to be an old pony at the Arran Riding School.

"Don't hit her! Oh, don't hit her!" cried Jinny, dashing forward to the pony's head. "She can't go any faster. She's too old, too tired."

At the sound of Jinny's voice, Brenda turned and came trotting to the end of the ride.

"What's up?" she snapped.

"Can't get this brute to move," said the man.

"He was hitting her," said Jinny, "and she's tired and old and shouldn't be working. She should be retired."

Brenda reached down and grasped Easter's rein. "Keep your legs back," she said sharply to the man. "You kick behind the girth not in front of it. And as for you, Miss Busybody, buzz off with you and mind your own business."

"It *is* my business . . ." began Jinny, but Brenda, urging her own horse forward, was dragging the white pony with her.

As Jinny watched helplessly, Easter turned her head to look back at Jinny, looked straight at her with wise dark eyes. As vividly as if Easter had spoken, Jinny knew that the pony was asking for help, asking Jinny to rescue her.

Jinny stood stock-still, watching the ride trail away from her. The moment of communication with the pony had been direct, undeniable, as if there was no such thing as sight known to humans and for a split moment Jinny had been able to see.

"It's all your imagination," said Petra's voice in Jinny's head. But Jinny knew it wasn't. The white pony had asked Jinny to save her, to free her from the torments of the riding school.

"I will, of course I will," Jinny promised. "I'll find a way. Even if I have to steal you, I'll find a way to rescue you."

There was no one at Glenbost to meet Jinny.

"Abandoned I am," she thought and, shrugging her shoulders, she began to walk to Finmory. Her mind was full of plans to save Easter, to bring her back to Finmory. "She can share the field with Shantih and Bramble. It wouldn't cost any more. Dad couldn't object. Maybe they'd be glad to let her come here."

"We've been looking for a good home for her, somewhere where she can retire. Thank you for taking her," said the Brenda in Jinny's head. But when Jinny thought about the real Brenda, with her painted mouth and hard, calculating eyes, Jinny had to admit that it wasn't very likely. "If I don't save her, they'll work her until she dies," thought Jinny, and saw Easter collapsing in the road, fighting to get to her feet again, then, exhausted, letting her head sink back into the gutter

Again Jinny saw the quick, urgent turn of Easter's head, saw, as clearly as if the pony was standing in front of her, the lips pulled back by the rusty bit, the hard leather of the bridle biting into her skin, her skull almost visible under the harsh coat, and again Jinny experienced the desperation that pleaded from the dark eyes. Again Jinny saw the pony as she must once have been, vibrant with life and energy, red rosettes flickering from her bridle as she was cantered round the show ring.

"I swear," said Jinny, "I swear I'll save you. And bring you to Finmory. I'll find a way."

When Jinny reached home she left her schoolbag at the stable and went straight down to Shantih. Ken was sitting by the gate, Kelly lying beside him.

"I hosed her leg for you," Ken said, pushing open the gate for Jinny. "Had a few soothing words with her."

"Thanks. That foul man kept me in for ages. I was going to start and hose her now," said Jinny, suddenly feeling too worn out to do anything except flop into an armchair, eat her supper and go to sleep.

Shantih limped across the field to Jinny, hardly able to put her foot to the ground.

"She's worse, isn't she, and the vet doesn't seem to know what to do next. He only said hosing wouldn't do any harm. Not as if he thought it would cure it."

"Give her time," said Ken gently.

"Time's no use if she's getting worse," stated Jinny, as she ran her hand down Shantih's neck and, stooping, picked up Shantih's lame foreleg. There was no swelling and no heat. Not a thing to show what was causing the lameness.

The chestnut Arab blew gustily over Jinny's head.

"What's wrong with it?" demanded Jinny. "What's wrong with your foot?"

But Shantih only flurried her nostrils again and nudged Jinny for titbits.

As Jinny straightened up she had the spine-tingling sensation that someone was watching them from behind the hedge.

Suddenly, Kelly, barking madly, scorched across the field. He charged at the hedge, lips wrinkled up from his teeth, his hackles raised.

"Kelly," shouted Ken. "Come back!"

But the dog fought his way through the hedge. At the other side, his barking changed to a deep growling.

"Kelly, come back!" Ken commanded.

Unwillingly, growling and grumbling to himself, Kelly came back.

"There was someone there," said Jinny, fear of horse thieves springing full-blown into her mind. "I felt them too."

But although they searched around the hedge and looked across the fields that reached down to the sea, there was no sign of any intruders.

"Probably only rabbits," said Ken.

"He doesn't get worked up like that about rabbits," said Jinny.

"Angels in disguise, then, waiting to be entertained, and we've driven them away?" said Ken.

Jinny ignored his suggestion.

"There was someone there," she said. "I'm sure there was."

CHAPTER FOUR

That night Jinny hardly slept at all. When she did fall asleep it was only to dream of Shantih, Bramble and the white pony being led away by night thieves to be sold to a racehorse trainer, who forced them to gallop endlessly, round and round the Grand National course. Screaming, Jinny would wake herself up, but each time she fell asleep again the same dream was waiting for her.

Twice she crept down to the field just to make sure that Shantih and Bramble were safe. The second time, her father was waiting for her.

"Where have you been?" he demanded crossly.

"To make sure Bramble and Shantih are still in their field," muttered Jinny.

"It is half-past two in the morning. Get back to bed and stay there."

"We told you there was someone lurking behind the hedge tonight. Kelly went for them."

"Ken said it was only rabbits," replied Mr. Manders, shepherding Jinny upstairs. "Kelly would know if there was anyone suspicious. He'd give the alarm."

"He gave the alarm and none of you listened to him," said Jinny, climbing back up to her room. "Fat lot of use having a guard dog and when he barks saying it's only rabbits. Bet he feels like Little Dog Turpie."

"Bed," said her father. "And stay there till the morning."

"I will do," said Jinny. "Even if I hear the hobyahs carrying you off."

For the rest of the night, Jinny tossed and turned restlessly. Once she got up, went through to the other half of her bedroom and stood in front of the Red Horse.

"Cure Shantih," Jinny murmured. "Make her foot better."

But tonight the Red Horse was only a painting on her wall. Its yellow eyes stared back blankly at Jinny. No spirit charged it with the strange power. Jinny was speaking to herself.

"And the white pony. Help me to save the white pony,"

38

pleaded Jinny, but the painting remained only a painting.

"Pretty faded, too." Jinny thought as she turned away. "I'll need to repaint it."

But she knew she wouldn't. Several times before, Jinny had planned to repaint the Horse, but when she had actually stood in front of it with her paints and brush she had been unable to touch it. Mr. MacKenzie had told her that once the Red Horse had been painted on a stone at Finmory's gates and every spring the tinkers had repainted it.

When the stone was blown up by the owners of Finmory who were making more flowerbeds, the tinkers had come in the winter when the house was empty, and a girl with long red hair, like Jinny's own, had painted the Red Horse on the wall, while an old woman of the tinkers had watched her. "Moaning and chanting while the lassie was painting the Horse on the wall," Mr. MacKenzie had said, remembering it from his unbelievable boyhood.

"Maybe that is the only way it can be repainted," Jinny thought, as she went back to bed. "Only the tinkers can do it."

At six o'clock Jinny decided that it was most definitely morning. Now it was daylight she could see Shantih and Bramble grazing safely in their field but, nevertheless, Jinny felt a vague sense of unease. Stray wisps from her dream still wandered through her mind and she couldn't shake off the certainty that there had been someone watching them last night.

She dressed and went out into the still, early-morning world, the grass heavy with dew, the grey sky washed with primrose and violet lights, the mountains beyond the moors bulked against the luminous morning light.

Filling a bucket with pony-nuts, Jinny took them down to the horses. At her approach, Bramble came bustling to the gate, smelling the nuts.

"You don't need any," Jinny told him, pushing past him to get into the field.

"I'm starving," exclaimed Bramble in sharp pig-squeals of greed, as he swarmed round Jinny trying to wedge his face into the bucket.

Jinny tipped half the nuts on to the grass and left Bramble suctioning them down while she went to feed Shantih.

The Arab blew over the bucket then picked out one or two nuts and rolled them round her mouth fastidiously,

39

swallowed them, then rested her head on Jinny's shoulder.

"Why are you still lame?" Jinny asked her, as she pulled Shantih's ears and scratched along the root of her mane. "What is wrong with your foot? Oh, why can't you tell me what's wrong? The vet's coming again this morning—fat lot of good that will do . . ."

Suddenly Jinny knew that this time there was someone watching her. She didn't turn round but went on talking to Shantih.

"Why can't he find out what's wrong? If you hurt your foot when you jumped, why isn't it better by now?" Jinny mouthed, wishing she had Kelly with her.

She heard Bramble swing round, positioning himself between the intruder and his few remaining nuts. Straining her ears, Jinny could just make out the light, almost silent footsteps coming towards her. In Shantih's dark eye she could see the reflection of a small figure walking towards them. It was too small to be a man and yet it didn't look like a child.

Jinny sprang round. "Tam!" she cried, and dashed across to where the tinker boy was standing. "How super to see you again. I thought you said you were all going away, that you wouldn't be back here?"

The tinker boy stood without speaking. He was about nine years old, a pick of bird bones draped in a man's jacket and old jeans cut short to fit him. His white face was sugared with dirt and his greasy hair was tucked back behind his ears. He stared straight at Jinny from eyes so black that she could see no pupil in them, only an intensity of purpose.

"Are you back staying at Alex McGowan's farm?" Jinny asked, wishing Tam would speak. "How's Zed?" she tried, asking for Tam's dog.

But still he only stood, fixing Jinny with his commanding collie eye.

"Would you like a cup of tea?" Jinny asked. "Some breakfast? I'm just going in for mine. Come on, come with me."

The boy flinched away. For a moment, Jinny thought he was going to make off without telling her why he was there. She put her hand out to catch his arm and the boy ducked away from her, lifting his arm to shield himself from an expected blow.

"Don't be silly. I'm not going to hurt you," said Jinny. But she had seen Jake, the man of the Brodie tinkers, knock a young woman to the ground. She knew why Tam had cringed away from her.

Last Easter, when Shantih and Bramble had been stolen, Tam, risking Jake's fury, had come to tell Jinny where to find the horses. If it hadn't been for Tam's courage, Jinny knew that she would never have seen Shantih or Bramble again.

"What's wrong? What can I do for you?"

Tam knitted his lips together, twisted his fingers.

"You've got to help me get her out," he said, the words, hard stones, painful to utter.

"Who? Get who out?"

"It's the old woman, Keziah. They've got her and locked her in."

"Prison?" demanded Jinny. She remembered the old woman she had seen when she had ridden to the tinkers' camp; her eagle-face and thick, steel-grey hair; the strength in her claw-like hand when she had gripped Jinny's knee, trying to force her to buy wood-chip flowers.

"The old woman I saw at your camp? They couldn't put an old woman like that in prison."

"In the hospital," said Tam.

"Is she ill? She must be if she's in hospital."

"She heard her call," said Tam. "She knows it's her time. Yon woman from the Social came. Brought an ambulance and took her off."

"You mean she's dying?"

"Aye."

"Then she's better in hospital. That's the best place for her if she's very ill," said Jinny. "Honestly."

"We've got to get her out."

"But they'll be trying to cure her."

"She's ninety-two. She's ready to go, but she'll no die shut in there without her folk round her."

"But where could she go? You mean back to your camp?" Jinny remembered the broken-down vans and black tarpaulin hump that had been the tinkers' camp. "Back to Jake?"

"Naw," said the boy. "He's gone off. Left her. Keziah said I was to tell you."

"Tell me? But what can I do? You can't leave hospital

until the doctors let you out. And where would she go to if she did get out?"

"You said you'd help me. You said to come and ask. Well, I'm asking."

"I will help," said Jinny. "You saved Shantih and I will help. I promised. I want to help, but what can I do.?" Jinny saw Tam, the old tinker woman and herself standing in a busy Inverburgh street. Keziah, still wearing a white hospital gown and wrapped in a flannel dressing gown.

"She said to bring you to see her. Will you come? Aye?"

"When?" asked Jinny, shrinking from the thought of going into the grim Inverburgh Hospital; knowing in her heart that she was afraid of seeing the old tinker woman. In Jinny's life, people were either alive or else you heard they'd died. You didn't visit them, knowing they were dying.

"Today."

"Not this morning," said Jinny. "The vet's coming to see Shantih. She's lame, but the vet doesn't know what's causing it."

"Aye." Tam agreed. "Come this afternoon."

Excuses skipped through Jinny's mind. "Jinny Manders," she told herself severely, "I am disgusted with you. You promised you'd help Tam—anything, anytime, and here you are trying to wriggle out of it."

"O.K." she said.

"Three o'clock. That's when they let you in."

"Outside the hospital?"

"Aye," said Tam, and he swung round and ran across the field.

"Don't you want some breakfast?" Jinny shouted, but he ignored her, running faster, diving through the hedge at the place where Kelly had barked last night.

It was after eleven before the vet came. Jinny had haltered Shantih and was grooming her at the kitchen door when she heard his car coming down the drive.

"And about time too," she said to Shantih. "If I miss the half-past one bus I'll not be at the hospital to meet Tam. He'll think I'm not coming." Knowing how easily she could miss buses when she didn't want to go somewhere, Jinny was keeping a close watch on the time.

"Any improvement?" asked Jim Rae, coming to stand

beside Shantih, running his hand down her shoulder.

"None," said Jinny. "And I've hosed it night and morning. Every day."

"It's worth trying. Still, can't say I've much hope. Run her up for me again."

Jinny did, but after a few strides the vet stopped her.

"We know it's her foot," he said, and yet again examined Shantih's hoof—tapping the hoof wall and the sole, pressing her frog. "Doesn't seem to feel a thing."

"But she does when she's walking. She feels it then," said Jinny urgently. "No good saying she doesn't feel anything when she does."

"A twist or a strain should be showing signs of clearing up by this time. Need to have it X-rayed. See what that shows up."

"And what will that cost?" asked Mr. Manders, coming to the kitchen door.

"The vet smiled ruefully. "Transports the thing. She'll need to go up to the Vet College in Glasgow. Nearest place.

"Cost a mint," groaned Mr. Manders.

"I've another horse going up. One of Danny Sargeant's prize Clydesdales. Got a kick on the shoulder. Fractured the bone and been standing in for six months. Needs to go back up for an X-ray in about a fortnight. I could arrange for Shantih to go with it. Danny'll not mind. You could share the cost."

"Sounds a good idea," said Mr. Manders, looking at Jinny. "Will it make any difference, Shantih having to wait?"

The vet shook his head. "May have cleared itself up by then. These mystery lamenesses sometimes do. And if it's the worst, time won't make any difference."

"The worst?" asked Mr. Manders. "You mean it may be something you can't cure?"

"Could be a fractured bone in the foot, and you can never rule out . . ."

The vet, catching Jinny's desperate expression, stopped himself in mid-sentence.

"But no point in worrying ourselves about these things until we get the result of the X-ray."

"You'll fix it up then?" said Mr. Manders.

"Will do," said the vet. "Though I'm quite sure Danny will be delighted to share the costs."

Jinny stood with her arm over Shantih's withers, feeling

the warm, strong bulk of her horse. Alive. Now. Shantih. The horror of the journey to the Vet College, the X-ray, the waiting to find out, to be told. Jinny shook back her hair, squared her shoulders.

Suddenly she remembered that she had to ask the vet if he knew the Arran Riding School.

"Mr. Rae!" Jinny shouted. "Wait a minute."

Leaning out of the car window, hand on the wheel, Jim Rae waited.

"Do you know the Arran Riding School? The horses are in a terrible condition. Absolutely dreadful."

The vet frowned and nodded. "So Martin Post's back to his old tricks is he? Used-car dealer by trade. The stables are a profitable sideline, and I dare say he uses them to fiddle his income tax. About two years ago, Miss Tuke got the R.S.P.C.A. to him. They took him to court, almost lost his licence, but he promised to clean the place up. Bought a few better horses, got rid of the worst ones. Wasn't too bad after that. I expect he's slid back into his old ways. If I'd anything to do with it, that Martin Post would never be allowed near another animal in his life."

"Martin Post?" Jinny said, "I thought it was a woman called Brenda something who owned it?"

"Is that what the current one's called? Been dozens of girls doing all the work for him. Lured by the thought of a cottage to themselves. I blame the idiots who pay him money to sit on his old crocks as much as anyone. I'll give you a phone when I've fixed up for the Vet College. Bye."

Jinny watched his car purr down the drive. She would need to phone the R.S.P.C.A. and tell them about the white pony, tell them that if they rescued Easter she could give her a good home.

"Jinny," called her mother. "If you're going to catch that bus, you'll need to get a move on."

"Double oats," Jinny promised Bramble, as she trotted in to Glenbost. He glowered, switching his tail. "I know you're mad," she told him, running her hand down his shaving-brush mane, "but it's no good sulking. I don't want to go any more than you do. But we've got to, so come on."

The bus was a half an hour late reaching Inverburgh. "Tam will think I'm not coming," Jinny told herself, as she scuttled through the hordes of Saturday afternoon shoppers crowding the pavements. "I know. I saw you," Jinny said, scowling furiously at a driver who had sounded his horn at her when she made a road detour round a crowd of boys. She ran on, panicking in case she should be late, desperate to reach where she didn't want to go.

As the soot-blackened walls of the hospital came into sight, Jinny slowed down, her flesh clinging more tightly to her bones at the sight of the high-barred windows through which she could glimpse hospital beds and screens; the stone steps leading up to the Ionic columns and on into the hospital itself. For a moment she couldn't see Tam and then she spotted him standing close to one of the columns, looking like a small, terrified animal crouching at the roots of a tree.

"Hi," said Jinny. "Bus was late. Do we just go in?"

Tam nodded but didn't move.

"Come on then," said Jinny, trying to sound as if walking into hospital was no more to her than walking into Finmory kitchen. "I expect she'll be pleased to see you." And Jinny marched on up the steps and pushed open the swing doors.

The hospital smell leapt out at her, hitting her with a wave of fear.

"Don't be a fool," she told herself. "Nothing is going to happen to you. You're only going to visit an old woman." "An old dying woman," mocked an echo in Jinny's mind. "Don't," Jinny warned herself. "Don't let it start." But it was too late, all the other things that she was worrying about came bursting out. The fear of the X-ray; the thought of the white pony that somehow HAD to be rescued from the riding school; and the thought of school where her last visit to detention meant that some time next week the Headmaster would want to see her.

"Well, don't just stand there," Jinny said, turning on Tam. "Come on, we'd better see her now we're here. Do you know which ward it is?"

Tam, cowering into his jacket, shook his head.

"Then we'll have to find someone to ask." And, holding the basket of fruit which her mother had given her for Keziah well in front of her, Jinny pushed open another swing door and marched down a brown, tiled corridor, Tam scuttling in her shadow.

CHAPTER FIVE

"And where are you two off to?" asked a woman in a green overall who didn't look much like Jinny's idea of a nurse. She thought her mother would have things to say about her fingernails.

"We want to see Keziah Brodie," said Jinny.

"You're far too young to be in here by yourselves."

"We've got permission," said Tam.

"And who gave you permission?"

"The doctor," said Tam, fishing a dirty-looking piece of paper out of his pocket. "He said I could come. There's nobody else to visit her."

The woman took the paper, holding it disdainfully between fat thumb and fat finger, and read it. She blew down hairy nostrils and handed it back to Tam. "In my day, rules were rules. Children stayed outside. Ward 29 you want." She pointed down the corridor. "Turn to your right at the end. Up the stairs. Left, then right again. Ward 29. And don't go poking your noses in. Ask if you can't find the way." Turning, she flapped off on flat feet.

"Come on," said Jinny. "Before someone else tries to stop us."

Jinny led the way down the long corridor, looking straight ahead, trying not to look past the curtains that half covered entrances to the wards, trying not to see the medical posters stuck on the walls, or the torture machines parked in alcoves. She found the stairs, climbed up them, looking through leaded windowpanes over the city streets.

"To be shut in here. To be waiting to die . . ." thought Jinny, and wanted to turn and run, back to Finmory, to feel the wind and the sun, to breathe fresh air again.

They turned left, along the corridor, then right.

"This is it," said Tam. "I know it now."

Written above an archway was "Ward 29". Jinny breathed in hard and pushed past the curtain that hung from the arch. She found herself in a long ward, the beds arranged along the walls on either side. For a second Jinny thought that nearly all the beds were empty and then she realised that the old women lying in them were so thin that their bodies were invisible under the bedclothes, only their heads sunk back on the pillows showed that the beds were occupied. Here and there sat a few palsied visitors.

Jinny didn't know what to do next. She stood awkwardly, trying not to stare at the parchment skins, gaping mouths and white wisps of hair. They were like skulls and Jinny couldn't keep her eyes away from them.

"Hulloa there," said a breezy voice, and a nurse came out of a doorway behind them. "Can I help? Looking for someone?"

"Oh yes," said Jinny, her relief sounding in her voice. "We've come to see Keziah Brodie."

"Why, that's right. I've met Tam." The nurse beamed down at them. "Keziah will be really pleased to see you. She's in the day room. I'll take you there." And the nurse walked down between the rows of beds, opened a door at the end of the ward, crossed a passage and opened another door. "In here, that's it."

The day room was a small carpeted room. At one end, a gaudy colour television set blared out a full-blast commentary on a football match. Grouped around it in a semi-circle sat half a dozen old women. Two were droolingly asleep; the others sat in a drugged dream, staring from themselves into nothing, their fingers knitting and knotting, their lips working, their bodies twisted by age into grotesque shapes.

Jinny was back in the yard of the riding school. She felt the same hopelessness, the same empty endurance as she had felt from the riding-school horses. But these were people. Some day her mother? Some day herself?

For a moment Jinny wondered which of them was Keziah. Not one of them looked the least like the old woman Jinny had seen at the tinkers' camp. Then Jinny saw her. She was sitting alone, staring through a barred window. Her back was erect, her steel-grey hair drawn away from the strong profile of her face; her lips were firm, her tanned skin deeply wrinkled. Despite the destructive noise of the television, there was a stillness, a silence in Keziah Brodie. The other old women had reached an end, were worn out, their days over. They had taken refuge from the reality of pain and the fear of death, had abandoned themselves to this doped infancy. But Keziah Brodie looked from herself with the assured air of a traveller about to start on an eagerly-awaited journey.

"Look who nurse has brought to see you," said the nurse, in a pink marshmallow voice quite different to the voice she had used when she had been talking to Jinny and Tam. "Isn't that nice now? There now, we'll feel so much better now we've got visitors, won't we? Someone to chat to? There now. That's my girl. Ups-a-daisy we go."

The nurse fussed around, straightening the rug over Keziah's legs, easing her up in the chair, tidying back her hair. But Keziah paid no attention to her.

"You'll hear the bell when visiting's over," the nurse said to Jinny. "You're rather late. Not much time left." And with a brisk tidying up of two of the other old women she left the room.

When the nurse had gone, Keziah slowly turned her head, her dark eyes set in their web of wrinkles acknowledged Tam and Jinny.

"You'll be the lass from Finmory," she said. "Tam brought you then."

"Yes," said Jinny. "How are you feeling? Mum sent you this fruit. She hopes you'll be much better soon."

"I'm ready to go," said Keziah, brushing aside the polite froth of Jinny's words. "The call will be for me in a week or two. I know that well."

"Oh no. Don't say that. You'll get better. That's what hospitals are for—to help you to get well."

Keziah laid her claw-hand on Jinny's arm.

"But before I go, there's one thing still to be done. Tam told me you gave him your word to be helping him when he was asking?"

"That's right," said Jinny. "I did."

"Then it is now we're needing you. You have to get me out of this place. It was only them with their interfering that brought me here. I'm helpless now with my age upon me. It's you must arrange the car to take me to Jock MacKenzie's. He has the bothy on the hill. He'll not be refusing Keziah Brodie the use of it."

48

"Oh, but you couldn't. Couldn't possibly leave hospital and go to live in Mr. MacKenzie's bothy. It's only a ruin. No one's lived in it for years. And you have to stay in hospital. They'll be treating you. You can't just leave," prattled Jinny anxiously.

"And where would the pride of Keziah Brodie be if she were to die in a place like this?"

"But you're warm here and comfortable," said Jinny in her mother's voice.

"Never to breathe the free air again, never to see the hills or the sea. To die without my folks around me. I see it in your eyes that you know the truth of it." The old woman's hand tightened on Jinny's arm.

"But aren't you having tablets and pills and things? You can't just stop taking them."

"Their filthy poisons," said Keziah, and she spat contemptuously on to the turquoise carpet. "I've cured myself all my days with the herbs of the hill. What would I want with their poison?"

"You just can't do that. You have to take medicine. You have to stay in hospital."

The grip of Keziah Brodie's talons bit into Jinny's arm. "You with the red hair and knowledge of the Red Horse speak the truth that is on your heart."

Jinny felt herself forced to look straight into the old woman's eyes, her gaze drawn to meet Keziah's. The voice she spoke with was her own true voice.

"I couldn't bear to be shut away in here. It's a foul place. I don't know how anyone ever gets well in places like this. There's no air. Just being here makes me ill. I couldn't bear it. Not to die in here and never breathe the hills again. I'll find some way of getting you out."

"Tomorrow," demanded Keziah. "Come and take me away tomorrow."

"Well . . ." began Jinny. "I'll try . . ."

"You'll tell Jock MacKenzie to be expecting me."

"Yes, but . . . I'll need to arrange a car. And I'll need help. I really don't know if I'll manage to get you out tomorrow."

The bell for the end of the visiting time shrilled through Jinny's fumbling excuses.

"Be bringing Maggie with you," Keziah told Tam. "She'll have the care of me for the few days I'm on the hill."

49

"Please," warned Jinny. "Don't get too worked up about it. Honestly, I may not manage to get you away tomorrow. There's a lot to be arranged."

"You must be taking me out of here tomorrow. I have the work that must be done."

"Well . . . I will do my best, but . . ."

"Ah, still here," said the nurse, coming in to make sure that Jinny and Tam were getting ready to go.

"Weren't you the lucky girlie to have two young friends to visit you like this," the nurse twittered. Then, without warning, she stepped forward, grasped Keziah's nose tightly between her finger and thumb, tipped back the old woman's head and dropped a red and black capsule into her mouth. Deftly she held Keziah's mouth firmly shut until she had swallowed the capsule.

Jinny stared, utterly appalled. She wouldn't have given Kelly a pill like that, not without speaking to him first, explaining to him what she was going to do.

"Come along now. Off with you," the nurse said to Jinny and Tam.

Keziah had turned from them and was again staring out of the window, distant and remote, a stillness upon her as if the assault had never happened.

"Don't worry," said Jinny. "I will be back tomorrow. I promise."

They found their way out of the hospital and Jinny organised Tam into a café.

"We've got to get her out tomorrow. She can't be left in there," Jinny told Tam when they were each seated in front of a glass of orange. "I've got to find someone to help. You weren't much use at all. Never opened your mouth, did you?"

"I couldn't be talking to Keziah. It was only yourself she had the eye for."

"Well, you'll need to buck up your ideas tomorrow," Jinny told him. "We'll need a car to get her to Mr. MacKenzie's. No good asking at home. Mum would have a canary at the thought, and Ken can't drive."

Suddenly Jinny thought of Nell Storr. She'd help. Nell owned a gift shop in Inverburgh. Not a trashy, tartan-touristy place but a special shop, more like an Aladdin's cave than a shop. She only bought things directly from the craftsmen who made them—weavings, carvings, jewellery, embroideries, paintings and pottery. When the Manders had first come to live at Finmory it was Nell who had encouraged Mr. Manders and Ken by selling their pots, and even now that Mr. Manders' first book had been a huge success he still made pots for her. She sold Jinny's pictures as well, was always looking for more, but Jinny wasn't very keen on giving them to her. Once a painting reached Nell's shop, Jinny never saw it again.

"I'll ask Nell Storr," Jinny told Tam. "We'll go and ask her now. I'm sure she'll understand and she's got a car."

"I'd better find our Maggie," said Tam. "Keziah will need someone to mind her. She'll be mad at me if I don't get Maggie."

"It's not absolutely sure that I'll get it all organised," said Jinny, faltering under Tam's certainty. "The car's one thing, but we've got to make them let Keziah come with us."

"The likes of them wouldn't be stopping Keziah," said Tam.

He stood up in a swift, furtive movement.

"You'll be there tomorrow?" he said, and with a quick duck of his head, Tam fled the café.

To Jinny's relief, Nell Storr was in her shop.

"Ah, Jinny. Joy to see you," cried Nell, flinging her arms around Jinny. "Weeks since I've seen you."

"Shantih's been lame," said Jinny, recovering from Nell's embrace. She felt the tightness that had cramped vice-like on her head begin to ease under the warmth of Nell's presence. Today Nell's hair was striped brown and blonde and plaited in a myriad of tiny plaits. She had glitter sprinkled on her eyelids and high cheekbones and two jade earrings hanging from one ear. Her nails were painted gold and she wore a scarlet kaftan, wide and flowing, caught in at her neck, wrists and ankles. Heavy gold and jade chains hung round her neck.

"So that's why you're looking so wretched. Ken did tell me, but I forgot. Still, I've got ten pounds for you. Money for your last two pictures."

"Oh, thanks," said Jinny. "Really it's not Shantih I'm worried about. Well, I am worried about her, terribly worried all the time, but that's not why I'm here. I need help."

"Wait a mo," said Nell. "Mrs. Lindsay, keep an eye on things. I'm going to brew up." Leaving her assistant in charge, Nell took Jinny into the back of the shop

"Herb tea," she said, giving Jinny a steaming mug. "Ken's been getting at me. Now, how can I help?"

Jinny blurted out her story while Nell listened intently.

"Are you sure she is dying?"

"She's positive. Says there's work she still has to do and only a week or two left. We can't leave her there. We must find a way to get her out. All her life she's lived outside and to be shut in there . . ." Jinny spread open her hands. "We can't leave her there. We can't."

"If there's nothing more they can do for her we'll take her out," said Nell confidently.

"We'll need a car."

"No problem. I'll pick you and Ken up about twelve tomorrow. You'll need to speak to Mr. MacKenzie. Make sure she can go to his cottage."

"It's not," said Jinny. "Just an old ruin. But if it is where she wants to go . . . How will we get her out of the hospital? Say they won't let her go?"

"Must do," said Nell. "Can't keep you in against your will. She can sign herself out."

Jinny sat beaming at Nell, a smile stretching her face. It all seemed so much easier now that Nell had understood, now that Nell was on their side.

Nell smiled back, her ugly, honest face strong and comforting.

"That's fixed then. See you tomorrow. Now I'll need to go, or Mrs. Lindsay will be having a sit down—as in strike, not chair."

"Thanks very much," said Jinny.

"Feel free," said Nell.

Jinny was just about to leave the shop when Nell called her back.

"Hey, don't forget your cash. Ten pounds," she said, giving Jinny two five-pound notes. "And I'd like some more drawings whenever you feel you can spare a few."

"Thanks," said Jinny, pocketing the money but not committing herself about the drawings.

Outside again, a clock in a bank window said five past four.

"The story of my life," thought Jinny. "Doomed to wander the streets of Inverburgh until it's time for a bus. Still, 'spose I might as well go and try to see Easter again. This time I'll wait. If she is out on a ride, I'll wait until she gets back then give her the apples."

Feeling rich, Jinny bought two pounds of the juiciest-looking apples and a pound of spring carrots and, crunching an apple, walked smartly out to the riding school.

When she reached the yard, a ride was getting ready to go out. Two young women were mounted on Sporty and Queenie, and a girl of about twelve years of age was making feeble attempts to haul herself on to the chestnut pony while he swung away from her each time she got her foot into the stirrup. A little girl in brand-new riding kit was clutching the reins of the 12.2. dark brown pony in her brightly-gloved hands and, to Jinny's dismay, the man she had seen riding Easter was standing at her head, obviously waiting to mount.

"No!" screamed Jinny silently. "No!" She wanted to dash forward and drag Easter away from the man. To shout, "You're far too heavy for her, you and your whip. Leave her alone. Can't you see she's worn out? Can't you see all she wants is a warm stable at night, and days of rest and sun? Can't you see?"

But Jinny bit the words back. If she made a fuss, Brenda would only order her out of the yard. It wouldn't stop the man riding Easter.

Brenda came into the yard talking to a man walking at her side. He had a smooth face as if his features were sinking into melting mounds of flab and his greasy hair was gradually being pushed off his head by the fat. He was wearing a tight navy-blue suit, pointed leather shoes, and from his double chins sprouted a red tie painted with a go-go dancer. He didn't look to Jinny as if he was going to ride.

"I'll be back on Tuesday to check over the books with you," he was saying to Brenda as he turned to go, making Jinny wonder if he was the Martin Post that the vet had told her about. His tiny pigs' eyes smeared over the neglected yard, the wretched horses, the riders, and inside his mounds of fat Jinny could almost hear the mini-computer checking up their value. He was Martin Post. He was the man who made money from this misery. And Jinny knew that nothing but money, the kind of money Jinny didn't have, would ever make this man part with Easter while she still had the strength to go on carrying customers on her back.

"Oke," said Brenda, and as the man turned to go, she came across the yard to take her horse from a girl who was holding it for her. On her way, she stopped to hold the chestnut pony's head while the girl, almost pulling the saddle over the pony's back, at last managed to mount.

"Get up, Mr. Broadbridge," she said to the man with Easter. "Let's get going."

The man grabbed his reins, pulling back Easter's mouth in a cruel grimace, the toe of his booted foot gouging against her ribs as he tried to mount.

Jinny knew what she was going to do. She ran across to Brenda, taking one of the five-pound notes out of her pocket as she ran.

"Please, please can I come for a ride. I'm sorry I'm so late. It was the bus. I've just got here. Look, I've got five pounds. I sold one of my paintings for five pounds!" Jinny tried to make it sound as if it was the most absolutely tremendous thing that could ever happen to anyone. "When I got the money I came to see if there might be the chance of a ride."

Brenda's lightless eyes stared suspiciously at Jinny. "Aren't you the one who rode last Saturday instead of Joyce? You're that kid who was making all the fuss over Easter."

"Only because I think she is such a super pony," enthused Jinny desperately. "She's the one I want to ride."

"You're too late," said Brenda. "We're ready to go now."

"Oh, please, please. Of course I realise that when you want to ride a special pony you have to pay more. That's why I've brought five pounds. That's what I'd expect to pay to pick the pony I want to ride."

Brenda checked over her shoulder, making sure that Martin Post had gone. She plucked the money from Jinny's hand and stuffed it into her anorak pocket.

"Bring Beech out," she said to a group of children who were hanging around the stable doorway, and to the man with Easter, "Swap over, will you? This kid's crazy to ride Easter. You take Beech."

"Oh. Right. I don't mind as long as it's got a bit more life in it than this stubborn brute."

Jinny dumped her apples and carrots in a doorway and took the iron-hard reins from the man. "You're welcome," he said. "I reckon it's spurs that one's needing. She's bone-idle if you ask me."

Jinny said nothing. She ran her hand over the blade of Easter's withers and down over her flat bony shoulder and concave neck. Gently, Jinny smoothed her face, feeling the skull under its thin covering of harsh coat, the great hollows above her eyes. The pony's eyes were nearly closed, the corners of her lips cracked, her nostrils drawn back, even standing in the yard her breathing was distressed.

"Sweet pony," murmured Jinny. "It's all right. There the pony. There Easter." A lump choked in Jinny's throat. Tears of fury filled her eyes. She dug her nails hard into the palm of her hand to stop herself crying.

"Don't stand about," shouted Brenda. "Get on." And Jinny realised that the man was mounted on the moth-eaten Highland and Brenda was looking down from the back of her bay.

"Can't you get on? Here, Wendy, help her up."

"It's O.K." snarled Jinny, and lightly swung herself up on to Easter's back.

"Keep her up with us," Brenda instructed, as she led the ride out on to the golf-course lane.

As Easter moved forward, Jinny could hear her bones creaking together, could feel the excruciating effort of each step the pony took.

"Oh Easter," mourned Jinny. "Easter." She hated Martin Post, hated Brenda, hated everyone who paid to ride Easter. Hated their total lack of awareness, that they could be so blind to such obvious suffering.

Jinny followed the ride for two or three minutes, then she took a deep breath and let out a loud groan. She slumped forward on Easter's neck, heard the man on Beech shout to Brenda and heard the bay horse being cantered towards her.

"Now what's wrong with you?" demanded Brenda.

"I think I'm going to be sick," said Jinny, and she slid slowly to the ground and stood with her head against the saddleflap.

Brenda waited an impatient minute.

"Are you all right?"

"Bit better," croaked Jinny, in what she hoped was the voice of someone struggling not to be sick.

"Well, stay there," said Brenda, "till you feel better. You can join us when we come back."

"I couldn't ride," gulped Jinny.

"Then take her back to the yard," snapped Brenda. "And don't you ask for your money back. You paid for your ride and that's that."

Jinny waited until they had ridden away then she straightened up.

"There," she said to Easter. "At least you can have a rest for an hour."

She loosened the webbing girth that was gummy with sweat and hairs; took off Easter's bridle, holding her by the loop of the reins over her neck.

"Wouldn't you like some grass? Looks super grass at the edges here. Bet you don't often get a chance to eat grass like that." And Easter began to snatch greedily at the green turf.

"Better take you back to the yard," Jinny said after a minute or two. "Before they see us. I've brought apples for you, and carrots, and I can take your saddle off there."

"Have you a halter?" Jinny asked one of the girls in the yard after explaining why she wasn't riding. The girl brought a halter.

"I'll take her tack off," said Jinny. "Does she go into a field?"

"Easter? At night she does, but we do evening rides on a Saturday. I expect she'll be going out on them so leave her in the third stall."

"Where's the field?" asked Jinny. "I'll hold her there until the ride comes back."

The girl pointed to a path. Collecting her apples and carrots, Jinny led Easter along it, to a smallish field, foul with droppings and almost as bare of grass as an Inverburgh street.

When Jinny opened the paper bags, Easter pricked her ears, her eyes brightening.

"All for you," promised Jinny, halving an apple and holding it out to Easter.

The pony lipped the apple from Jinny's hand and stood mumbling and mouthing it until it fell on to the ground.

"Come on," encouraged Jinny, picking it up and holding it out again.

When Easter took it from her this time, Jinny realised what was wrong. She had expected the pony, being old, to have the long teeth of an aged horse, but Easter was so old that her teeth were worn down.

Jinny bit the apple into little bits and fed them to Easter. She ate them greedily, pushing at Jinny's hand for more, her ears pricked and her eyes bright.

"When you're at Finmory," Jinny promised her, "I'll make special food for you—bran mashes with treacle, flaked maize and boiled oats. You can have whatever you want. And no more work. Never, ever again will you have to cart people about. You can have a rest with Shantih and Bramble for company."

Almost as if she understood Jinny's words, Easter lifted her head. Her dark eyes looked straight at Jinny and, for a moment, the wave of communication passed between the pony and the girl.

"I'll rescue you. I'll phone the R.S.P.C.A. tonight, and if they won't do anything, I'll come at night and take you home with me to Finmory. I promise."

But although Jinny phoned the R.S.P.C.A. four times that evening there was no reply.

"Flippin' closed for the weekend," muttered Jinny, banging down the receiver.

"Who are you trying to phone?" asked her father.

"Oh, nobody," said Jinny vaguely, not wanting her parents to know what she was planning just in case the R.S.P.C.A. weren't interested and she had to rescue Easter herself. "It doesn't matter."

She went to bed to toss and turn, thoughts of Shantih, Easter and Keziah boiling in her mind.

CHAPTER SIX

Jinny woke early the next morning, dressed quickly and went out to Shantih. The Arab came limping to meet her.

"I'll hose you now," Jinny told her. "Then I've done it. Today is going to be one of those days."

Shantih danced at the end of the halter rope, her neck arched, head high and tail kinked over her back. After her weeks in the field she was wild to escape, to be galloping over the moors again. Her trumpeting whinny rang out to the mountains.

"Shut up! You'll wake them all," Jinny warned, trying to hold on to the halter rope with one hand, while she aimed the jet of water at Shantih's lame leg with the other. "I'm only doing it so I feel as if I am *doing* something instead of only staring at you. I don't really suppose it will cure you. The vet doesn't think it will. Why can't he find out what's wrong. Why?"

Jinny had been meaning to ride Bramble down to the farm, but Bramble said he would like a day in his own field, if it was all the same to Jinny.

"Only to get the milk," Jinny assured him, but Bramble, turning his quarters on Jinny, said he did not believe her and would she stop bothering him and leave him alone.

"Be that way," said Jinny, and set off for the farm on foot.

On the Sabbath the old farmer milked the cows, then changed into his Sunday black and attended church in the morning and evening. Much to Jinny's relief, he was still working about the yard when she reached it. Asking him about the bothy would be tricky enough without disturbing him when he was getting ready for church. Jinny didn't know what would happen if Mr. MacKenzie said no.

"It's yourself," Mr. MacKenzie said. "I was thinking it might be when I saw the early worms careering past. That horse of yours still lame? I'm thinking it will be the bullet for her." His sharp eyes in their spearmint sockets quizzed Jinny from the shadow of his cap. "A relief to you it would be to be rid of her."

"Milk," said Jinny, clattering down her can. "And when you've filled it, I have something very serious to ask you."

"Is that so now," said Mr. MacKenzie, and went to fill Jinny's can.

"Now, let's be having your very serious request."

"You know the tinkers? Well, the old woman, Keziah, is in Inverburgh Hospital. She's dying. I went to see her yesterday and it's a terrible place. So hot you can't breathe, and stinking, and she's stuck in there with all those other doped old women, and nurses bossing her about. It was terrible."

"Aye, it's a bad business. I was thinking Keziah Brodie would be dying with the open sky above her, not in yon killing bottle. It's the terrible hard life she's had, and a bonny woman she was in her day. Not a farmer that didn't set his cap at her for all she was a tinker lass. But she was true to her own folk. One of the last of the true tinkers before they were eaten by the greed like the rest of us."

"She wants to get out," said Jinny, her hopes rising at Mr. MacKenzie's words. "She told me to ask you if she could come to your bothy. Tam and someone called Maggie will look after her. She said there's something she must do before she dies."

Mr. MacKenzie sucked on his short-stemmed, blackened pipe and stared out over the moors. Jinny waited in silence. She knew Mr. MacKenzie would make up his mind and that would be that. He was not one to be persuaded. Her parents had been most unsympathetic about the whole business, Mrs. Manders repeating all the arguments about why they couldn't possibly bring a ninety-two year-old woman out of hospital and leave her in a bothy.

"If she is as seriously ill as you say," Jinny's father had said, "she's probably on drugs. You can't suddenly take her out. What will you do if she's in pain? Real pain? In hospital they can stop that pain. Can't do that if she's left in that old ruin."

But Ken had understood. He'd pushed his long, bony hand over his eyes and forehead as he listened to Jinny.

"I'll be with you," he'd said. "If I had my way, I'd close all hospitals."

"And when *you're* ill? When *you* need doctors and hospitals? What then?" asked Mr. Manders.

"All the money they spend on their insane bombs and weapons. I'd take it all and build sanctuaries where the sick would be made whole. Places of love, so that even to be in them brought wholeness. Where people could discover who they are."

"Nell's coming about twelve," Jinny had said quickly, to stop any of her family telling Ken that he was talking impossible nonsense. For what was nonsense—the way the world ran things, or Ken's visions?

"I'll be there," Ken had said.

"Aye," said Mr. MacKenzie at last. "She can come here if she has the mind for it. I'd not be turning her away, though it's the tinks will be swarming over my land like the locust when the old yin dies."

"Oh, thank you," breathed Jinny. "We'll bring her here this afternoon. Thank you."

"Aye. I'll take a wee walk up to the bothy myself and be leaving them a few things."

During the morning, Jinny had tried the R.S.P.C.A. number three more times, but still there was no reply. By the time Nell Storr arrived at midday, Jinny had given up hoping for an answer. She had decided that they really must close down for the weekends.

Nell was driving a low-slung Bentley, not Jezebel, her own sports car.

"What a car!" exclaimed Jinny, as she and Ken climbed into its vastness. Normally Jinny thought of all cars as killers and could hardly tell the difference between a Mini and a bus.

"Rather dishy," agreed Nell. "Borrowed, naturally, but better than Jezebel for bringing home the ancient."

"Now," said Nell, when they were purring along the road to Inverburgh, "Plan of action—first we must see her doctor. Then, if it seems at all possible, out she comes. They can't stop us. She can sign herself out."

Tam and Maggie—a young woman with jet-black hair—were waiting for them at the hospital steps. Maggie was dressed in a smart suit and high-heeled shoes. She stepped forward to meet them.

"Good afternoon," she said. "Tam's told me you think you can bring Keziah out of hospital. I'm Maggie McVake, Keziah's great-niece."

Jinny introduced her to Ken and Nell.

"And I'm Jinny," she added.

"Aye. If Keziah has the mind to be finishing her days in the bothy, I'll come and see to her. It's a few years now since I was living in the open, but I'll not care if it's what the old one wants."

Jinny, who had been expecting Maggie to be someone younger but much the same as the other tinkers she had met, couldn't help feeling relieved. Even her mother would approve of Maggie.

They walked up the hospital steps together; Nell, in a fringed black dress, high boots, and with a scarlet and gold shawl over her shoulders, and Ken in his usual black sweater and faded jeans, going first. Then came Maggie and Jinny, with Tam walking in their shadow. Ken pushed open the swing doors and the hospital smell engulfed them. With a shudder, Jinny imagined how it would have been if there had only been herself and Tam. Walking behind Nell and Ken, Jinny felt protected and secure.

"Which way to Keziah?" Nell asked, turning to Jinny, and Jinny stepped up beside them leading the way.

"Remember this feeling," Jinny told herself. "Remember this when you're rescuing Easter. When you feel like this, people can't stop you. Be afraid in yourself and that's when things go wrong. When you're afraid, you're wanting people to stop you."

"Visiting is not for another half-hour," a nurse told them when they reached Ward 29. "You'll have to wait outside."

"Could I see the Sister?" said Nell. "We want to see the doctor who is looking after Keziah Brodie, but I think we had better have a word with the Sister first."

"You must have an appointment to see a doctor."

"Nonsense," said Nell. "There isn't time for that red tape."

"You must have an appointment. You certainly can't demand to see a doctor on a Sunday afternoon."

"What's the trouble, Nurse?" demanded a full-blown, official woman in a blue uniform.

"They want to see a doctor about Keziah Brodie."

"I'll deal with it, Nurse."

"Right, Sister." Casting curious glances over her shoulder, the nurse padded away down the ward.

"Now, what is this disturbance all about. I cannot have shouting in my ward."

"Words, man, words. Let the silence be," murmured Ken.

"We've come," explained Nell, "to take Keziah Brodie home. This isn't the place for her."

"Are you aware that Keziah Brodie is a dying woman?"

"Oh yes. This makes it all the more important that we take her out today with as little disturbance as possible."

"I think," said the Sister in acid tones, "you had all better come into my room till we sort out this nonsense," and she led the way into a small room.

"Now, tell me first of all who you all are."

"This is Mrs. McVake," said Nell briskly. "She is Keziah's great-niece who will look after Keziah, and this is Tam, Keziah's grandson. We are their friends. We're here to help them and unless there is a valid reason why Keziah should not leave the hospital we're here to take her home."

"Keziah Brodie is dying. At the most she has a fortnight to live."

"Yes," said Nell firmly. "We know that and she has the right to choose where she will spend her last days."

"I utterly refuse to consider your taking Keziah away."

"We wish to see her doctor," stated Nell.

For seconds, the Sister and Nell glared eyeball to eyeball. Electricity zizzed between them. Jinny dug her nails into the palms of her hands, clenched her teeth in support of Nell. Ken moved, almost imperceptibly, forward. The Sister held her ground, battallioned behind the power of her uniform and her ridiculous little headdress.

"If you please," said Nell.

"There is absolutely no question of Keziah Brodie leaving this hospital today."

Nell's silence waited unmoved, commanding.

"But if you insist on wasting Doctor's precious time . . ." the sister shrugged contemptuously. She picked up a phone and asked for Dr. Gupta to come to her room.

"Thank you," said Nell, as the sister replaced the receiver, ignoring them.

In the minutes of waiting, Jinny felt the hospital smells reach to the very marrow of her bones. She hated the regulated rows of beds, the power of the uniformed men and women, and the white-coated doctors who knew things you didn't want to hear.

"It'll be like this at the Vet College," Jinny thought, "when I'm waiting to hear the result of Shantih's X-ray. Please God. Please God, let her be all right. Let me be able to ride her again."

There was a light tapping on the Sister's door, and an Indian doctor with little hands and neat feet in patent-leather shoes twinkled in.

"Are you having trouble?" he asked, smiling about him. His glinting eyes unfocused.

The Sister explained the situation. "And of course I have already told them that the whole thing is out of the question," she finished.

"Indeed yes. She is a very, very, old, done woman. No more we can do, I am most sorry to say."

"But we can take her home?" insisted Nell.

"I would not advise that course of action. I could not give my sanction for such a foolhardy act."

"She wants to die in her own place," said Ken.

"In my own country we would understand this wish, but here it would not be allowed to take her away."

"No medical reason why she should not come with us?" asked Nell.

"As I have said, she is a very old lady . . ."

"Far too ill for you to remove her," snapped the Sister.

"She will sign herself out," said Nell, her words in the future tense, her tone of voice stating something that had already happened.

A nurse brought in Keziah in a wheelchair. She sat erect and proud, her gnarled hands folded on her plaid rug, her hawk-eyes hooded.

"It is my wish to leave this place," she said, when the doctor explained to her that if she signed the book discharging herself and left against the hospital's advice she would not be readmitted.

"This is no place for me," stated Keziah, her eyes fixed beyond the confines of the room, beyond the prison walls of the hospital to where the winds scoured the bleak moorlands that she had loved all her life.

When they brought the book, Keziah signed it with a firm hand. She was free to go.

The nurse wheeled Keziah out of the room, then a short time later wheeled her back dressed in her own clothes. Ken took the wheelchair.

"The responsibility is entirely yours," said the Sister. "You are removing a dying woman from the only place where she could be properly looked after."

But as they took Keziah down in the lift, she didn't look like a dying woman. She looked like a queen coming again into her rightful kingdom.

Keziah dozed for most of the journey back to Finmory, and when they reached Mr. MacKenzie's yard, the farmer was waiting for them.

"Aye, Keziah," he said, opening the door of the car. "You've come to visit me."

"I have so. And it's grateful I am to you for the use of your bothy."

"Aye," said Mr. MacKenzie solemnly. "You be having the use of it, but keep those thieving fingers away from my eggs and my hens."

"Never did I touch the least feather of one of your hens and I'd sooner be supping the arsenic than be putting one of your eggs to my lips."

Jinny grinned with delight. She caught the fleeting shadow of a smile brush over Tam's pinched face. It had worked. They had rescued Keziah. She was back with people who spoke her own language, who knew her.

Mrs. MacKenzie insisted that Keziah came in for a cup of tea before she went on to the bothy.

"I've put some things up for you," she told Maggie. "And be sending Tam down for milk and eggs as you're needing them."

"It's good of you," said Maggie, "but I'll be paying for them. I've a fine man now. No need for charity. It's only for Keziah's sake that I'm back on the hill."

"There now," soothed Mrs. MacKenzie. "I'm seeing for myself the change in you—but don't be too proud to ask for help if you're needing it."

Ken, Nell and Mr. MacKenzie supported Keziah along the stony track that led to the bothy. Although, wrapped in her swaddlings of dark clothes, Keziah appeared a tall, strong woman, Jinny could tell from the way they helped her over rough patches of ground that she must weigh little more than a child, and once, when they had to cross a burn, Ken swung her into his arms and carried her easily across it.

The bothy was a small, two-roomed cottage that had once been used by shepherds who worked on the farm. Now one gable wall had collapsed, the rusty corrugated iron that was tied over the roof clanged in the wind. The glass of the windows had long since fallen to the ground and been overgrown by nettles. The outside door stood open. Running ahead of the others, Jinny looked in and saw that one of the rooms was still reasonably intact. A peat fire glowed in the open hearth; on a broken-down bed-settee were blankets and pillows; two buckets of water stood by a large pan and a blackened kettle, and a wicker basket was full of milk, eggs, bread and vegetables. On the wooden floor was a thick woollen rug, and two other old chairs stood against the wall.

"To have somewhere like this," Jinny thought longingly, "of my very own. Where I could ride and paint and no one to bother me."

She ran across the room and looked out at the back of the bothy. There was a small overgrown garden, then about an acre of land fenced off from the hill, the grass in it growing lush and sweet.

"For Easter," thought Jinny at once. "She can come here. Mr. MacKenzie will think she belongs to the tinkers. Mum and Dad don't need to know anything about her—least, not straight away." It seemed almost too good to be true.

They settled Keziah on to the bed-settee, wrapping the blankets about her, putting pillows at her head. The old woman sank back, her eyes closing, the bone in her beak nose sharp, her mouth sunken. For the first time, Jinny saw the resemblance between her and the other dandelion-headed women they had left lying flat and thin in their regimented ward.

"Best leave her to herself," said Maggie. "I'll be here."

For a moment, Ken and Nell stood looking down at Keziah.

"I'll be pleased if I ever make half the woman she is," said Nell.

"Aye, she's the bold one," said Maggie. "Many's the battering I've had from that one."

"Anything else you need?" asked Jinny.

"No," said Maggie. "It's fine we'll be now. Thanks to you all."

Keziah opened her eyes, fixed her dark gaze on Jinny. "It's well you've done by me," she mouthed. "It's the true word you have." Her eyes closed again, her hands relaxed and she slept.

"The minister will not be holding back his sermon for the likes of her," said Mr. MacKenzie. "I'll be going, or the church will be without one of her finest singers this night."

Nell went with Mr. MacKenzie to where she had left the car in his yard, while Ken and Jinny made their way back to Finmory. As they reached the house they saw a van parked at the door.

"The Tuke," said Ken, recognising Miss Tuke's Pine Trekking Centre van.

"Thought she was too busy trekking to be bothered with me," Jinny grumbled. "Wonder what she wants?"

Mr. and Mrs. Manders, Mike and Miss Tuke were all sitting round the kitchen table, empty coffee mugs in front of them and the remains of one of Mrs. Manders' cream sponges in the middle of the table.

"At last!" exclaimed Miss Tuke, pushing back her chair and slapping her palms on her jodhpured knees. "Been waiting for you. Come along."

"Come where?" said Jinny in amazement. "To have a look at Shantih? I thought you were too busy trekking to care."

"Well, you were wrong. Had a look at your nag when I got here. Could be anything. Get her X-rayed. See what that shows."

After the high of bringing Keziah out of hospital and taking her safely to the bothy, Miss Tuke's words were clouds suddenly blotting out the sun. Desperately Jinny wanted Shantih to be sound again, ached to be riding her, galloping over the sands, but she was terrified of the X-ray, terrified of what it might reveal.

She twisted a strand of hair through her fingers, not looking at Miss Tuke, half listening to Ken telling her parents what had happened at the hospital.

"So we'll go now," finished Miss Tuke.

"Go where?" demanded Jinny, suddenly realising that Miss Tuke had been speaking to her.

"Always suspected it," said Miss Tuke, speaking to Mr. Manders. "Your younger daughter is bananas, clean loco. Now, listen this time. We're going to the Arran Riding School. Heard from Jim Rae that you'd been hanging round the place and were pretty shocked. It's a year or two since I checked up on that Post character. Last time we crossed swords he nearly lost his licence. So come along, we'll take another little look round."

Jinny grabbed the last piece of her mother's sponge and hurried after Miss Tuke. In no time they were rattling down the road to Inverburgh.

"Let's hope it's not as bad as you think," said Miss Tuke, when Jinny had finished describing the state of the riding school. "But knowing Martin Post, anything is possible, and the worst, probable."

CHAPTER SEVEN

Miss Tuke swung round the lane leading to the riding school, jammed on her brakes in front of Brenda's cottage and bounced out of the van.

"We'll have a recce round first," she announced, striding down the path to the stable yard.

Two girls were sitting in front of the looseboxes sharing a picnic of sandwiches and lemonade, but apart from them the yard was deserted. Hands on hips, Miss Tuke glared around.

"Absolutely filthy. Total neglect," she said loudly, as her gaze took in the fouled concrete, the fungused dung swept into corners, the scummed water trough and the broken-down buildings.

She turned on her heel and marched across to the looseboxes. Queenie and Sporty were in the first boxes, Brenda's bay and the chestnut pony were in the other two. All the animals were still tacked up and damp with sweat from their day's work. Only the chestnut pony had the energy to lift its head to look at the strangers. It was obviously days since the boxes had been brushed out.

"Are you looking for Brenda?" asked one of the girls. "Do you want to book a ride?"

"How long," demanded Miss Tuke, "have these poor brutes been standing there? And why on earth is their tack still on?"

"We never take it off between rides," said the girl. "Brenda says it's not worth it. They'll be going out again at seven."

"How many rides have they done today?" asked Miss Tuke.

The two girls looked at each other uncertainly.

"The men's ride in the morning—that's a two-hour ride—and three rides this afternoon," said one of them.

"Five hours," said Miss Tuke grimly. "And they're going out again?"

"Oh yes. It's always very busy at the weekends. There's always night rides."

"I don't suppose," said Miss Tuke, "that you bother to feed them? Live on air, do they?"

"They get hay at lunchtime, and Brenda used to give them hay just now but Mr. Post caught her. Told her they didn't need it, not when they'd all that grass."

"What grass?" said Jinny. "I've seen their field and there's no grass at all."

"How do you know?" asked one of the girls suspiciously. "What business is it of yours, anyway?"

Miss Tuke ignored her and strode across to the doorway that led to the row of stalls where the rest of the ponies stood in a weary line.

"Can't believe it," said Miss Tuke, as she walked down the row of ponies. "How anyone could work animals in this condition! I'd shoot the man myself. The brute."

Furiously, Miss Tuke kicked the bales of mouldering hay piled at the end of the stalls.

"And if that's what she's feeding them she needn't bother."

"This is Easter," said Jinny, going up to Easter's head. "She's the white pony I was telling you about."

"Poor old woman," said Miss Tuke, casting her experienced eye over the pony. "You've come down in the world, haven't you?"

Miss Tuke ran her hand gently down Easter's neck. "You're quite right," she said to Jinny. "She has been a beauty once."

"Bet she was a show pony," began Jinny, and she was on the point of blurting out how she planned to save Easter and bring her back to Finmory, but for once managed to stop herself in time, to remember that it was Miss Tuke she was speaking to.

"I don't suppose," said Jinny cautiously, "that there is anything you could do for her now? She's too far gone, isn't she. I mean if, just if, I could take her home and feed her up it wouldn't make any difference, would it?"

"Rubbish," said Miss Tuke briskly. "She must be as tough as old boots to have survived this place. Given a chance she might pull through."

Jinny's face lit up at Miss Tuke's words.

"You mean it?" she demanded. "Really mean it?"

Miss Tuke had stopped thinking about Easter.

"Come along," she said. "Let's get weaving. We're off to see Martin Post. Put the fear of death into him and get this shambles cleared out."

When they got back out into the yard, Brenda and the two girls were coming to meet them.

"Can I help you?" said Brenda, sounding as if help was the very last thing she was likely to offer.

"Dear girl," said Miss Tuke, "the only way you could help me is to start and get this place gutted. Get some food into those horses, get them groomed, shod and cancel all rides for the rest of the summer and see . . ."

"Just a minute," interrupted Brenda, "this is a private yard you're in, and before I listen to any more of your interference—get out."

"Oh, we're getting out. Straight out and straight to Martin Post's. That's where we're going, and unless he gets this dump cleared up in the next few days, private yard or not, you'll be having a little visit from the R.S.P.C.A. my dear."

Before Brenda could answer, Miss Tuke and Jinny were across the yard and making for Miss Tuke's van.

Crashing gears, foot hard down, Miss Tuke drove like an avenging fury to Martin Post's detached bungalow where it stood in landscaped splendour in the shrubbed outskirts of Inverburgh.

"That girl's bound to have phoned him," said Miss Tuke, as they got out of the van. "No point in trying the front door. We'll go round the back. Know the place well. Sunday evening our Martin will be entertaining his friends to drinkies. We'll give him drinkies!"

And with Jinny close behind her, Miss Tuke charged up the path and round the side of the bungalow.

Martin Post and five plastic people were sitting on a patio arranged round a table of drinks, looking like a T.V. commercial.

"Ha, ha!" snorted Miss Tuke, warhorse smelling battle, "so this is where you are! Slothing as usual. Excellent. You'll have plenty of time to listen to what I have to tell you."

The plastic people twittered uneasily—Miss Tuke was not the sort of person that should have appeared in their commercial—while Martin Post blubbered to his feet, a glass of gin in his hand.

"What the devil are you doing here?" he demanded.

"To warn you," said Miss Tuke. "Your riding school is in a worse state than it was when I saw it two years ago. I dare say you'll remember the outcome of that visit. Eh? Filth and neglect everywhere. Hardly a horse fit to work. Ponies that should have been put out of their misery months ago. If I'd had my box, I'd have brought the worst of them with me, made you look at them. None of my business what you do with your second-hand cars, but while I'm around you're not treating animals like that. I'll be round tomorrow with the R.S.P.C.A. and the police to investigate the place. And don't think a court will let you keep your licence a second time."

Miss Tuke swung round and began to stride away. Martin Post heaved his bulk after them, catching up with her at the front of the bungalow.

"Calm down," he said. "Cut out the hysteric female act. You're jumping the gun as usual. Not a thing wrong with the stables. Sunday evening, end of the weekend. Place is bound to be a bit untidy. It'll be cleared up by Monday morning."

"Pull the other one and it'll play Annie Laurie," said Miss Tuke contemptuously. "Horses miraculously renewed every Monday. Mouldering hay turned into best feeding. Full oat bins appearing out of nowhere. Good. Then you'll not mind a visit from the R.S.P.C.A.?"

"Give us a week. I'll get the place squared up by then. It's that girl's fault. Can't trust her to do a thing."

"And how much do you pay her, I wonder? Dare say that could do with a spot of investigating as well."

"Listen, give me a week, O.K. Then you can come and poke your nose in where you like. I'll grant you some of the horses aren't all they might be. I'll send the worst off to the knackers. Give the place the once over. How will that be?"

Since Jinny had rounded the corner of the bungalow she had felt as if she had been watching a play, a performance. Only now did Martin Post's words really reach her—"Send the worst off to the knackers."

"But not Easter," she cried. "You mustn't send Easter to the slaughterhouse!"

71

As if noticing Jinny for the first time, Martin Post focused his piggy eyes on her.

"Heavens," he said. "You don't think I know the names of the donkeys, do you?"

"The white pony. The one that used to be a show pony. You mustn't send her to be killed." .

"That old crock? It'll be the first to go." He laughed, his breath stinking in Jinny's face, watching her closely to see her reaction.

"You can't. Not Easter. Let me take her home. I've got a field where she can retire. I'll pay for her. Please let me have her."

Martin Post's thick lips drew back from his yellowed false teeth.

"Darling," he sneered, "If you were to offer me a thousand nicker for her, I wouldn't let you have her. Thursday morning the meat man will be there to collect her. There's a little thought to sweeten your dreams."

"Please!" cried Jinny.

"Please away," said Martin Post. "You don't think you can come here with that old hornet and expect favours from me?"

His fat hand reached out to pinch Jinny's cheek, and she sprang back just in time to stop him touching her.

"I'll give you a week," stated Miss Tuke. "Not up to standard by then we'll see what a court has to say about it. And you know I mean it."

All the way back to Finmory, Jinny sat without speaking, her mind full of plans to save Easter. She had thought that if the riding school was improved it would be the best thing for Easter, but it had turned into the worst. Now she must rescue her before Thursday or it would be too late.

"Would you drop me at Mr. MacKenzie's," Jinny asked as they approached Finmory.

Miss Tuke nodded and stopped at the farm to let Jinny get out.

"Don't start a nonsense over Easter," Miss Tuke warned. "Best thing for her to be put down."

"That's not what you said before. You said she'd a chance."

"More fool me. You can't save all the old ponies in the world. Not if you aim to stay sane."

"Think I'm mad already," said Jinny, as she got out of the van.

Jinny waited until Miss Tuke was out of sight then she made her way up to the bothy. Tam was sitting in the doorway. Jinny called him over.

"Listen," she said urgently. "I've helped you now you must help me."

Tam looked at her warily.

"You couldn't have got Keziah out of hospital by yourself, could you? And I organised it all, didn't I? Well, there's an old pony in a riding school in Inverburgh. She's been a super pony once but she's old now. They think they're going to slaughter her on Thursday but it's not going to happen. I'm going to rescue her."

Tam's face remained expressionless.

"I've thought it all out. We'll go on Wednesday night and take her away. We'll bring her back here and she can stay in the bothy field. They'll all think she's a tinkers' pony. No one will bother. You will help me, won't you?"

"Aye," Tam agreed unwillingly.

"Right. Wednesday night then," Jinny stated. "I'll give you the bus fare and we'll meet in Inverburgh after school."

Straight after school on Monday, Jinny went up to the bothy to see Keziah. The old woman was sitting up on a chair taking a plateful of soup. Jinny's heart lifted at the sight of her. They had done the right thing bringing her to the bothy; she was back where she belonged.

"Aye, she's fine," agreed Maggie. "We've had Jock Mac-Kenzie up cracking memories with her the whole afternoon."

When she reached home, Jinny told her parents that she was going to spend Wednesday night with a school friend who had asked her to her birthday party.

"Rather short notice," said Mr. Manders, "asking you on Monday when the party's on Wednesday."

"She did ask me before, but I said I couldn't go because of not being able to get back to Finmory. Then at the weekend her mother said why didn't I stay the night. So she asked me again today. I can go, can't I?"

"Yes, of course you can," said Jinny's mother. "You'll enjoy it."

Wednesday was the longest day that Jinny had ever

known. From the minute she woke up and looked out to where Shantih was standing resting her foreleg, the day dragged, second by leaden second.

"Have a nice time at the party," her mother said.

"Will do," said Jinny, drowning in guilt. "It's for Easter," she told herself, summoning up behind her eyes a vivid picture of the white pony. "If I don't rescue her, she'll be dead tomorrow.

Even double art, which always made Wednesday afternoons Jinny's favourite, dragged interminably. They were meant to be painting a jungle scene after listening to jungly music. Jinny was drawing Easter. She saw Mr. Eccles the art master, approaching and quickly flipped her paper over.

"Not started yet?" Mr. Eccles asked. "No jungle vibrations?"

Jinny shook her head without looking at him.

"Come on. Let's see what you've been drawing."

Reluctantly, Jinny turned over her paper.

"Surprise! Surprise!" said Mr. Eccles. "Horses!"

"Stubbs," said Jinny, as she always did when Mr. Eccles teased her about drawing horses. "And Munnings and Skeaping."

"And no doubt Manders, given a year or two. But now, how about a jungle. You may include a tapir if you wish."

Jinny didn't wish, but unwillingly daubed her paper with greens and browns and blues as she thought about the night ahead.

When the bell went, Jinny tore down to the cloakroom. She hurriedly changed out of the dress Mrs. Manders had considered most suitable for a birthday party, and into the jeans, sweater and anorak which Jinny considered most suitable for rescuing Easter. In her canvas shoulder bag, Jinny had a halter, food for Easter, her own torch, which wasn't as powerful as her father's and therefore less likely to attract attention, and all the money she had in the world—seventeen pounds from her box and the three pounds she had left from the money Nell had paid her on Saturday—just in case she should need it.

There was an hour before Tam's bus was due to arrive at the bus station. Jinny wandered round the streets staring into shop windows, then sauntering on, thinking all the time of Shantih and Easter.

So far the vet hadn't phoned about the arrangements for Shantih's visit to the Vet College and Shantih was as lame as ever—it was weeks since she had been sound, weeks since Jinny had been able to ride her, weeks since her disastrous fall. Over and over again Jinny had relived that jump—the moment when she had turned Shantih and ridden her at the wall.

"It's all moments," Ken had said. "If you can catch the moment and stop yourself then the rest doesn't have to happen, but if the moment gets away from you all the rest follows on."

Worry about Shantih was a stone in the pit of Jinny's being.

Tam was first off the bus, his eyes darting from side to side, searching for Jinny. When he spotted her waiting for him he dived to her side.

"Good," said Jinny, glad of even Tam's support. "I'm jolly glad you made it."

"Where's the pony?" asked Tam, as if he expected Easter to be tied to one of the bus shelters.

"Good bit from here, but we can't go to the stables until it's dark. We'll wait until we're sure that Brenda has gone to bed and then we'll find Easter and take her back to Finmory.

It was almost dark before they set off for the riding school.

"If Brenda sees us hanging around she'll guess we're up to something," Jinny had insisted when Tam nagged about the waste of time, but at last she agreed that it was dark enough.

They found a place in the golf-course hedge where they could hide and watch the light in Brenda's cottage windows.

"Ten past eleven," said Jinny, shining the torch on her watch as at last the cottage lights went out. "We'll wait till midnight. Brenda should be asleep by then!"

Tam, crouching on his hunkers, his man's jacket doubled round him, his arms crossed over his chest, his sparrow hands holding his shoulders, showed no sign of having heard Jinny. He waited without movement, as settled as an animal.

"Honestly," thought Jinny. "He's useless." She longed for Nell Storr or Ken to be with her. But Jinny knew that they wouldn't have come. What she was going to do she had to do herself.

"It's nearly twelve," Jinny announced. "It's now or never. Come on."

They got up, stretching numbed limbs, and crept along the golf-course lane, which led through a gate then between sheds into the stable yard. The smell of horses and dung filled the darkness.

"Right," said Jinny. "We'll check the boxes first."

But they were all empty. The weak pencil beam of Jinny's torch only picked out unswept stone floors and the cobwebbed shadows that textured the wooden beams. In one box, something that was much too big to be a mouse flowed across the floor and up the wall at the side of the manger. Jinny shuddered convulsively.

"Now the stalls," she said, trying to make her whisper sound full of confidence.

At first Jinny thought that the big double doors leading into the stalls were locked by a huge padlock. "If Easter's in there and we can't get to her . . ." thought Jinny, then realised that the padlock was hanging uselessly from the hasp of one door. They weren't locked at all. Jinny freed the clasp and began to inch the door open, the wood screeching against the stone floor.

"Gorn! You'll have her up," said Tam, and taking the door from Jinny, moved it slowly and silently until there was enough space for them to squeeze through. All the stalls were empty.

"Must all be in the field," muttered Jinny, quickly swinging her torch away from the bales of hay at the foot of the stalls that seemed to be alive with vermin. She swung round, pushed her way out and stood clutching at herself in the yard, while Tam silently closed the door.

"Our Jake, he'd batter you one for your din," said Tam.

"That's all we need," snapped Jinny. "Your Jake."

"He'd have had the pony away by now," sneered Tam.

"I dare say," said Jinny. "He's used to taking things but I'm not. Come on, they must all be in the field." Following the light of her torch, she led the way down the track to the field where she had held Easter on Saturday.

They climbed over the gate and stood peering into the dark.

"Horses, horses," called Jinny in a low voice. "Easter, Come on, Easter."

For a second there was no response. Only the darkness pressing tightly against them.

"They must be here," said Jinny, straining her ears.

Then she heard the sound of trotting hooves, high pig-squeals of anger, the unmistakeable sound of a kick finding its mark, and suddenly the riding-school horses were crushing around them, necks snaking, jostling, pushing; hind legs lashing out to keep other horses away; a sudden power of horses bursting out of the darkness. Jinny realised that they thought she was going to feed them. Tam clutched at her as Jinny, throwing up her arms, growling in as loud a voice as she dared, tried to drive them off. But they pushed closer, desperate for food. The whites of their eyes glistening, yellow teeth terrifyingly close, as for split seconds they were caught in the beam of Jinny's torch. The smell of the titbits Jinny had brought for Easter made them wild for food. Brenda's bay reared above Jinny. In the darkness she could hardly see it, was only aware of the bulk of horse balanced over her, then the crash of its hooves just missing her head as it plunged to earth again.

Holding Tam firmly by the arm, Jinny made for the gate. The horses stampeded after her. She pushed Tam over the gate first, then climbed over herself. Safe on the other side, Jinny stared at the cottage, waiting for a light to appear in the bedroom window, for surely Brenda must have heard the noise. To Jinny it had sounded like an earthquake.

But no light shone into the darkness. Brenda couldn't have heard. Gradually Jinny's heart slowed back to normal. The horses, abandoning the hope of food, began to turn away from the gate.

"Thought we'd had it," said Tam, his voice a thin bleat of sound. "I'm not for going in there again."

"We won't need to," said Jinny. "Easter wasn't there. The chestnut pony wasn't either. They must be somewhere else. There must be another field. We'll need to search for it."

They crept back to the yard and followed muddy paths that led to a midden, out on to the golf course, to a rubbish dump and to a rotted coal shed that had sat down years ago.

"The pony'll no be here," suggested Tam.

"Of course she's here. She must be here somewhere. I should have made sure I knew where to find her," said Jinny, as they stood in the yard not knowing where to look next.

"Had we no better be going?" asked Tam hopefully. "We'll not be finding her tonight."

Jinny was cold with terror; the terror that she was too late, that the meat man had come early and taken Easter away, that the pony she was searching for was already dead.

"There's a field by the side of the cottage," Jinny remembered. "The first time I came here I wasn't sure where to go. I saw it then. Come on."

Tam hitched up his jeans and followed Jinny along the track between the outhouses. When they emerged, Brenda's cottage seemed menacingly close.

"Say she did hear the horses?" Jinny thought. "Say she's standing now at one of the windows listening?"

Jinny pushed back her hair, squared her shoulders and forced herself to walk on. "As if Ken and Nell are in front," she thought. "Remember how it was walking through the hospital." But try as she would, Jinny didn't feel like that now. She felt scared.

Along the bottom hedge they went, and there was the tiny field Jinny had seen on her first visit to the stables. Oil cans and smashed poles were piled at the gateway, three twelve-inch-high jumps were standing in the middle of the field, and two pony shapes lifted their heads and stared curiously at the intruders. One was the chestnut pony and the other was Easter.

Jinny flung herself over the gate and stumbled across the rutted earth to Easter. For a split second as she stood, white in the darkness, Jinny saw her again as the show pony she must once have been—the delicate-boned face, the unblemished legs, the proudly-arched neck—but it was only an illusion. Jinny's hand stroked a harsh neck and sunken back. The days of Easter's triumphs were lost in the past.

Jinny dragged the halter out of her bag and put it on Easter, while the pony stood like a block of wood, almost without life.

"You're not going to be slaughtered," Jinny whispered. "You're coming home with me. We're taking you home."

Jinny shared out the titbits between Easter and the chestnut.

"There's a lot more for you at Finmory," Jinny promised. "And a field full of grass just for you! Come along, we're going home." The old pony moved stiffly as Jinny led her across the field to where Tam had opened the gate.

At the gate Easter stopped, and Jinny, turning to see what was wrong, shone the torch beam over Easter's wasted body, her scarred legs and sunken quarters. Seeing her like that, Jinny didn't care how wrong other people might think it was, taking Easter away when she belonged to Martin Post. Jinny hardly cared whether they called it stealing or not. Her one thought was to save Easter from the slaughterer, to take her home to Finmory and see her grow fit and well again.

On an impulse, Jinny buried her face in Easter's neck, throwing her arm over her withers.

"It's all right now," she whispered. "You're safe now."

"Here," grated Tam's voice. "Stop that messing. We've to be getting her out of here before we're nabbed."

Jinny roused Easter into reluctant life and urged her through the gateway. Then she turned, closing the gate.

As Jinny struggled with the bolt, her foot caught against an empty trough. For a moment she fought to keep her balance, then fell into the piles of rusty oil drums. With a reverberating crash the cans became alive, like rows of dominoes they sent each other rolling and banging, filling the silent night with thunderous din.

CHAPTER EIGHT

Jinny and Tam froze with terror. This time Brenda must have heard them. No one could have slept through such a commotion.

"Oh no you don't," Jinny cried, catching at Tam's sleeve. "You're not running off. I came into that foul hospital with you, so you're staying here with me."

No light appeared in the cottage. The silence of the night settled back. At the first crash of the falling oil drums the chestnut pony had high-tailed it to the other end of the field, but Easter had stood, hardly moving, while the cans rolled about her.

"Come on, then," Jinny said at last, and together they began to creep back along the hedge. Tam was silent as a fox, Jinny shuffling and stumbling with the sharp click of Easter's joints sounding like gunfire behind them.

When they reached the end of the hedge, they paused for a moment level with Brenda's cottage. Suddenly Jinny saw a figure standing half-hidden by the overgrown rambler roses of the porch.

"Look out!" she screamed, her voice ripping the darkness. But her warning was too late. Brenda leapt from the porch, grabbed Jinny's arm and the scruff of Tam's jacket.

"So it wasn't just the horses kicking the cans about," Brenda said.

Tam twisted from her, ducked expertly, and Brenda was left holding his jacket while Tam vanished into the night.

"Little blighter!" swore Brenda, tightening her grip on Jinny's arm.

Jinny scowled furiously up at her, Easter's halter rope held tightly in her clenched fist. She knew that she could probably wriggle free from Brenda and escape too, but if she did that it would mean leaving Easter behind; her last chance of saving her would be gone.

"Here, give her to me." Brenda prised Jinny's hand from the halter rope, left Easter standing at the doorway and, twisting Jinny's arm behind her back, frog-marched her into the cottage.

"Let me go," Jinny yelled, as Brenda forced her through a small hallway and into a stone-flagged kitchen.

"Stay there," Brenda ordered, pushing Jinny into a chair. "I'll deal with you in a minute."

Jinny heard the key turn in the kitchen door, the slam of the front door, and the sound of Easter's hoofs as Brenda led her back to her field.

Jinny stayed sitting in the chair, clutching her arms about herself, staring from her at the dim shapes in the unlit kitchen. She had failed to rescue Easter. Had mucked it all up. Now she was only another of all the humans who had let the pony down.

"Right then," said Brenda coming back into the kitchen, switching on the fluorescent light so that Jinny could see the dirty dishes piled in the sink, the remains of a meal spread on a table covered with a dirty, plastic tablecloth. An ancient fridge wheezed asthmatically, a calor gas cooker stood iced with grease, and an electric fire with one of its bars broken crouched in the middle of the floor.

"Here, I know you, don't I? You're the kid who made all the fuss to ride Easter and then was sick. And it was you nosing about with that old bag, wasn't it?"

Brenda switched on the electric fire and stood in front of it. She was wearing corduroy trousers rolled up at the ankles and a heavy sagging pullover. Her grimy, painted toenails poked through open-toed sandals. The make-up on her face had set, after a day's endurance, into patches of greasy colour, and her eyes were like a panda's black-rimmed with rubbed mascara. Her hannaed hair hung round her head in lank tails. She folded her arms and stared at Jinny through strangely dead eyes.

Jinny scowled back at her.

"Out with it then. What were you doing stealing one of my ponies?"

"I wasn't stealing her. I was rescuing her so that she wouldn't be sent to the slaughterer's tomorrow. I was going to pay you for her." Jinny scrabbled in her bag and laid her money on the kitchen table.

"That's all I've got just now, but I was coming back to find

81

out how much more you wanted for her. Honestly I was. I couldn't ask you before I'd rescued her. You wouldn't have let me buy her. And that rotten Martin Post who owns all this mess, he would do anything to stop me saving her."

"So you decided to steal her?"

"No! No! I had to rescue her. What difference does it make if I take her and pay you what you would have got for her from the slaughterhouse? But it would make all the difference to Easter. It would give her a year or two of peace and comfort. Just a bit of happiness at the end of her life. That's all I wanted."

Brenda listened without changing her expression.

"You don't care, do you? You're as bad as Martin Post. How can you work in a place like this? How can you? You don't care how cruel it all is as long as they make money for you. When did Easter last have a decent feed? When was she last groomed? Or her feet seen to? This whole place is the same. It stinks of dirt and neglect, and if Martin Post doesn't clean it up, Miss Tuke will bring the R.S.P.C.A. in and they'll make him close it down this time."

Suddenly Jinny couldn't go on. It was useless. Shouting at Brenda wasn't going to stop them sending Easter to the slaughterhouse tomorrow. Now she had been caught there was nothing else Jinny could do. She had failed. Easter was not to have her summer by the waters. This time tomorrow she would be dead, would be dog meat.

"But I hate you!" Jinny screamed. "I hate you!" Burying her face in her hands, Jinny burst into tears.

For a minute Brenda stood without speaking, then, slowly, she crossed the kitchen, filled a kettle and, setting it to boil, put instant coffee, milk and sugar into two mugs. She took a bottle of whisky from a cupboard and poured some of it into her own mug. When the kettle had boiled, she filled the mugs and took one over to Jinny.

"Here," she said, touching Jinny's shoulder. "Wipe up and drink this."

Jinny flinched away from her.

"You've had your say. I asked for it. Now you listen to me."

Reluctantly, Jinny pushed back her hair revealing her mottled face. She groped in her pocket and dabbed at her eyes and nose with the ineffectual remains of a paper hand-kerchief. Then, without looking at her, she took the coffee from Brenda and sat holding the mug in both hands.

"That's how it all looks to you, doesn't it, Little Miss Busybody?" Brenda asked, going back to stand by the electric fire, taking a deep slurp of her coffee.

"That's how it is," muttered Jinny.

"Not how it looks to me," said Brenda. "How old are you? Twelve? Thirteen? Well, I'm forty-nine. Remember tonight when you wake up and find you're nearly fifty. See what you think of it then." Brenda took another slug of her coffee.

"I'd never work in a place like this," stated Jinny. "Never."

"When I was your age I'd have said the same thing. But there we are—things change. Here, I'm more or less my own boss. Martin Post doesn't bother me much and I've got my own house. What would I be doing if I wasn't here? Working in a shop or an office, going back to a furnished room, or dancing attendance to a family that was rich enough to keep me along with their dogs, being bossed about by spoilt kids. No thank you. This suits me O.K."

"Don't you care about the horses?"

"Got used to them. They don't have all that bad a time. If I'd to choose, I'd rather be one of them than a showjumper—carted about, forced to jump impossible heights over and over again."

"But you can't *like* working here?"

"Oh, I'd fancy dreams of my own riding school. Or a Fell pony stud. But they're old photographs now. Faded. Pretty ridiculous really. It's O.K. here; a load of old crocks, I'll grant you that, but they suit the people who ride them.

"There's always one or two of the nags go to the knackers at the end of the summer, so they're only going a few weeks earlier than usual. What were you going to do with her, anyway? Keep her in your back garden? She'd have starved there all right."

"'Course not," said Jinny scornfully. "I live in Finmory House, past Glenbost. We've masses of grazing, and I'd got a special field for Easter. Super grass."

"I've been to Finmory Bay," said Brenda. "D'you mean that mausoleum where the hippies used to live?"

Jinny nodded. It didn't matter now.

83

Brenda turned to rinse out her mug, holding it under the tap, setting it down on the draining board. She stood staring at it then turned to face Jinny.

"How much cash have you got?"

"Twenty pounds."

"Martin will get eighty from the knackers. Could you get the rest in a month?"

Jinny heard Brenda's question but for seconds she couldn't make herself answer, for if Brenda was asking her that, did it mean . . .? Could it possibly mean . . .?

Jinny nodded furiously, for of course she would find the rest of the money somehow, some way, if it meant saving Easter.

"Will it be all right with your parents?"

Again Jinny nodded, unable to speak.

"Then you can have her. I'll tell Martin she's gone to a friend of mine who'll pay him the knacker's price for her. Always had a soft spot for Easter. Something about her."

Jinny sat motionless, staring dumbly at Brenda.

"It isn't true. It can't be true. I'll wake up and it will all be a dream," Jinny thought, digging her fingernails into her arm.

But nothing had changed. The dirty kitchen was still there. Brenda was still standing there, her mouth twisted into a wry grin as she watched Jinny.

"You mean," Jinny stammered at last. "You mean I can take Easter back to Finmory? Now? Tonight?"

"That's what I said."

"Oh, thank you! Thank you! I'll find the rest of the money, I promise, and there's masses of grass and plenty of food for her. Oh, thank you, Brenda."

"Don't thank me. I'm not doing you any favour. You'll never be able to make anything of her. She's beggered, that's for sure. Could drop dead in a week's time and you'll still have to pay me."

Brenda's cynical laugh cut through Jinny's delight.

What happened to make her like this. Jinny wondered suddenly. What changed her when once her dreams were almost the same as mine—her own riding school, her own Fell ponies.

"Don't," Jinny warned herself, and aloud she said, "Shall I go and get her now? Shall I just take her home?"

"Lord," said Brenda. "You weren't thinking of leading her all the way to Glenbost? Still, I suppose you were. I'll drive you over in the morning."

"I've to be at school," said Jinny.

"We'll leave early. Fiveish. You can crash down here for the night. What about the boy who was with you?"

"Tam!" exclaimed Jinny, jumping to her feet. "And you've got his jacket."

Jinny ran outside shouting for Tam. She ran down the golf-course lane, yelling his name at the top of her voice. There was no sign of him. She ran into the yard, still shouting. Tam, wrapped in sacks, appeared from one of the outhouses.

"Did she get you?" he demanded.

"It's all right," said Jinny. "Brenda's O.K. She's letting me take Easter. I've to pay for her, but she's mine. Come on in."

Reluctantly, Tam allowed himself to be persuaded into the cottage. He sat perched on the edge of one of the chairs, his dark eyes fixed on Brenda.

"You'll need to spend what's left of the night in here," said Brenda doling out horse blankets.

Tam took his and curled down on the kitchen floor. Jinny, wrapped in hers, tried to make herself comfortable on two chairs.

Even when the sound of Brenda going back to bed had faded into silence, Jinny's mind wouldn't stop galloping on. It whirled her from thoughts of Shantih's lameness to what Mr. MacKenzie would have to say about Easter occupying his field. "But he can't mind," Jinny thought. "He's not using it and it's only to begin with. When she gets a bit stronger, I can put her in with the others."

At five, the outside world was chill and grey. Jinny, going to catch Easter, found her standing close against the hedge, her eyes closed, her coat glistening with moisture. When Jinny spoke to her, she seemed to have to come back from a far place before she could lift her head and acknowledge Jinny's presence.

"You're coming home with me," Jinny told her, leading her out of the field. "It is true this time. It is happening now. You're mine. You'll never have to work again, never be hungry again."

The horsebox that Brenda had driven into the yard was as old as everything else at the riding school, but Easter went up the loose boards of the ramp without any protest. Brenda turned down Jinny's suggestion of hay for the journey.

"Don't worry," Jinny told Easter as she tied her up. "It wouldn't have been up to much, and there's a whole field of lovely sweet grass just for you, where you're going to."

Tam travelled in the box with Easter. Jinny sat in the front with Brenda. When they had safely negotiated the empty Inverburgh streets and were rattling along the road to Glenbost, Jinny broached the subject of paying for Easter.

"I'll bring you the rest of the money just as soon as I possibly can," Jinny said.

"You've a month. No longer. Remember that now," warned Brenda, her words shaking the ash from her lip-hanging cigarette all over Jinny.

"If I haven't got enough by the end of the month, what then?" asked Jinny, risking the unthinkable, for it was better to know definitely than to keep on imagining things.

"I'll come for her, take her to the knackers myself and give the money to Martin. Any longer than a month and Martin will start to smell a rat. If he finds out, there'll be hell to pay, especially when he doesn't want you to have her. Reckon he'll be around the yard a lot after Friday. He's away this week on business. Starting Friday, he's tarting the place up for Miss Tuke's inspection."

Jinny stared out at the barren countryside. The only way she had any hope of making eighty pounds was by selling pictures to Nell. Jinny had tried that before when she had been desperate for money, tried to draw dozens of pictures of Shantih, but because she had forced herself to draw them when she wasn't feeling like it they had turned out so badly that Nell had refused to take them. They would have to be better this time.

Brenda drove the box up to the gates of Finmory House.

"Straight through?" she asked Jinny.

"We'll take her out here and lead her over the hill. It's not far and it's a lovely field for her."

"I'll come with you," Brenda said. "I'll see her settled in."

Jinny led Easter along the sheep track that curved above Mr. MacKenzie's farm, then on to the bothy. It would have

been quicker to have parked the horsebox in Mr. Mac-
Kenzie's farmyard, but Jinny hadn't wanted to risk meeting
him. She would see him this evening and explain. Much
better than trying to explain at this time in the morning.

At first, Easter walked wearily at Jinny's side, but gradually, as they climbed the hill, her head came up, her eyes
brightened, and with pricked ears she began to look about
her. Her step quickened and once, for no reason other than
joy, she broke into a trot.

"It has been worth it," Jinny thought—all the hassle and
the explanations that still lay ahead; worth it even for these
few moments of seeing Easter coming alive again.

There was no sign of Keziah or Maggie. The bothy was
still closed against the world. Tam opened the gate of the
enclosure and Jinny led Easter in. She took off her halter and
stood back.

"On you go," Jinny said. "It's all for you."

Easter raised a foreleg and pawed at the grass; she lowered
her head and wuffled her muzzle through it. Then, with a
high-pitched whinny, she trotted forward, stood for a second,
then stiffly lowered herself to the ground, swung over onto
her back and scrubbed herself luxuriantly into the grass,
kicking her legs awkwardly into the air in an effort to roll. She
struggled to her feet, shook herself, then dropped her head
and began to graze.

"What are we standing here for?" Brenda demanded
hoarsely. "I've got a day's work ahead of me."

Reluctantly, Jinny turned to follow her, saw her sur-
reptitiously drag the back of her hand across her eyes before
she lit another cigarette.

"I'll come up straight after school," Jinny told Tam.

"Aye," said Tam. "I'll have my eye on her."

"And tell Mr. MacKenzie I'll see him this evening."

"Aye."

"All right for some," said Jinny. "He'll probably spend the
whole day watching Easter."

"You're not so badly off yourself," said Brenda, pointing
down to the field where Shantih and Bramble were model
horses from a child's toy farm. "Are they yours?"

Jinny explained. "But Shantih is lame," she finished
despondently, a little of her joy over Easter leaking away.

"She's been lame for weeks and the vet can't find out what's wrong. That's why I came to the riding school. I wanted to ask you if you knew what it might be."

"Then you saw the set-up and didn't bother to ask," Brenda said, finishing Jinny's sentence. "It figures. Still, tell me now."

Jinny did.

"Don't like the sound of it. You'll know definitely after the X-ray."

"The vet said it could be a hairline fracture in one of the bones of her foot."

"Could be," said Brenda dubiously. "It's a possibility. Bad enough if it's that. She'll be lame for life but the odds are she won't get any worse; you could keep her and breed from her. But if it's navicular, nothing else for it but . . ." and Brenda put her two fingers to the side of her head and clicked her tongue.

"What do you mean?" cried Jinny. "What do you mean, navicular?"

At the word, the brightness had gone from the morning. Navicular. The word chill as cancer in a human being. It seeped like poison gas into the very core of Jinny's being. Its cold fingers of dread clutched at her heart. When she had been reading through her horsy books trying to discover what could be causing Shantih's lameness, her eyes had flicked away from the horror of navicular. She had locked it away at the back of her mind with other unthinkable things. But Jinny knew exactly what her book had said. It had said: "Navicular—an incurable disease of the navicular bone in the forefeet."

White-faced, her nostrils pinched, her lips tight, Jinny turned on Brenda.

"Don't talk such bloody nonsense," she swore. "Of course Shantih hasn't got navicular. It comes on slowly. Shantih went lame suddenly. Of course it isn't navicular. Of course it isn't"

"Pardon me for breathing," said Brenda, shocked by Jinny's visible terror. "But surely the vet's mentioned navicular? He must suspect it when he's having her X-rayed. I know of a case where it came on suddenly. The nerve had been blocked, and when the horse landed heavily out hunting it went dead lame and it was navicular."

Jinny opened her mouth to tell Brenda that the vet wasn't an idiot, that of course he didn't think there was any possibility of navicular, and then she remembered how Jim Rae had stopped in mid-sentence. His voice echoed in Jinny's ears: "You can never rule out . . ." and then he had stopped suddenly and told her not to worry until they got the result of the X-ray.

At once there was no doubt in Jinny's mind. She was sure. He had been going to say navicular. Jinny shuddered uncontrollably. The joy of seeing Easter come alive again as she breathed in the freedom of the moors, had gone; it was less than a memory now.

"It couldn't, it couldn't be," said Jinny, staring at Brenda.

"Could," said Brenda.

"Do you think we could hurry or I'm going to be late for school," said Jinny's voice, empty, polite.

She couldn't bear to go on talking about Shantih. When the vet phoned with the date for the X-ray she would have to ask him if it could be navicular. He would say there was a chance—a chance that when they saw the result of the X-ray, some time in the future Jinny would have to say "Yes," say "Yes" to Shantih being put down; would have to be sensible about it because it would be the only thing possible.

"Please could we hurry," said Jinny again.

The bell for them to get into line was ringing at school as Jinny jumped down from the cabin of the box.

"You'll bring the rest of the money to the riding school?" Brenda said.

"Will do," said Jinny. "The very minute I have it."

"Jinny Manders!" exclaimed Dolina, as Jinny joined her line. "Would you be looking at yourself. Is it sleeping under the hedge you've been at?"

"Don't worry, I'm going straight to Miss Lorimer. 'Miss Lorimer,' I shall say, 'I've come to save you the trouble of hunting me down. My appearance is a disgrace to the school, my homework is undone and I expect I'll fall asleep in class. Please may I go to detention now?' "

"If you hadn't gone belting off last night you'd have seen Miss Lorimer then. She was looking for you. You've to go and see the Headmaster this morning."

CHAPTER NINE

When Jinny got off the school bus that evening, Mr. Manders was sitting in the car waiting for her.

"This is it," thought Jinny grimly, as she took the letter the Headmaster had given her to give to her father out of her schoolbag. "Here goes."

She walked across to the car and got in.

"Bus was on time tonight," said her father, starting up the engine. "How was the party?"

Jinny swallowed hard. "There wasn't a party," she said. "I made it up. It was all lies. I took Tam with me to the riding school. I was going to rescue Easter, but Brenda caught us."

"Oh, Jinny," said Mr. Manders, looking at his daughter's woebegone face. "Oh, Jinny." And he reached across, putting his arm round her shoulders, hugging her to him. "You crazy coot. You'll never learn, will you?"

"Doubt it," agreed Jinny ruefully. "But don't worry, I'm not for the juvenile court this time. In the end, Brenda agreed to let me have her. She's going to tell Martin Post that a friend of hers has taken Easter and they'll pay him the same money as he would have got from the slaughterhouse."

"How much will that be?" asked Mr. Manders, releasing his daugther.

"Eighty pounds. I've paid twenty and I've to give the rest to Brenda within a month."

"But you haven't got sixty pounds."

"I will have. I'll paint pictures for Nell. I'll get it somehow. I will."

"And where is the pony now?" asked Mr. Manders, abandoning the question of paying for Easter in the face of Jinny's certainty.

"Mr. MacKenzie's field. The one by the bothy."

"And does he know about it?"

"I'll see him tonight. If he's mad, I'll need to bring her down to our field. Don't really want to put her in there in case Bramble bullies her. You should have seen her when we let her go in the field. She couldn't believe it was true. All that grass to herself. She was quite different. Not old and wooden but young again."

"Put on its rose again," came into Jinny's head from a poem she had read, and she lit up inside. The miseries of the day, her interview with the Headmaster, the things Miss Lorimer had said to her were completely wiped out. For the instant, Jinny's whole world was white light, was joy.

"You should have seen her. If only you all could have seen her."

"It's quite good having you to tell me about it," Mr. Manders said, looking resolutely ahead through the windscreen.

"The next bit's not quite so good," said Jinny, deflating. "That's a letter from the Headmaster. I'd to go and see him today. I should think it's about me being in dentention so much and not working."

"Not at all good," agreed Mr. Manders. "We'll talk about it after I've read the letter."

"I think he wants you to check up on my homework every night. Sign it to say I've done it. Take an interest in me."

"I hope you told him that at least fifty per cent of Manders' family conversation is about you and your homework?"

Jinny didn't reply. She felt a small silence would help to change the subject.

"The vet phoned today. He said he'd spoken to Danny Sargent and they could take Shantih for the X-ray this Saturday or the next. I said this Saturday was out because we're meeting the Wrights, so we arranged the next. You've to phone him tonight, after nine, just to let him know that it's O.K."

"I'm not meeting the Wrights," stated Jinny positively. "I said when you got the letter from them that I wasn't coming. Petra was there, you can ask her. I cannot stand Belinda Wright. But the next Saturday will be best for the X-ray."

"If you're sure you're not coming to Inverburgh with us why not make it this Saturday? Get it over with. The sooner you find out what is wrong the better?"

Jinny shook her head. Once Shantih was X-rayed, Jinny would know. She wanted to put it off for as long as possible. Wanted it never to happen.

"Shall I go in and see Mr. MacKenzie now?" Jinny asked as they approached the farm.

"Better come home first. You can tell us what actually did happen at the riding school last night, and we'll see what the Headmaster has to say about you."

The Headmaster's letter was mostly about Jinny's in-attention in class and her undone homework.

"Right," said Mr. Manders. "What homework have you tonight?"

"English essay," said Jinny. "French sentences and a drawing of a stone-age village."

"Well, finish your tea and straight upstairs. When you've done all your homework bring it down and I'll check it."

"But I've to go and see Easter and Mr. MacKenzie and I've hardly spoken to Shantih. Couldn't I do it after I've seen them?"

"Certainly not," said Mr. Manders sharply. "Your school work is far more important than all this nonsense."

Subdued, Jinny went on eating her salad. Her mother had been most unenthusiastic about Keziah being left in the bothy. Although she had approved of Maggie when she had gone to see if there was anything she could do to help, she still thought that the best place for Keziah would have been hospital. And she had listened to Jinny's confessions with a serious face.

"How can we trust you when you do things like this?" she had said. "You're always telling us to leave you alone and then you do this sort of thing."

Mike went upstairs with Jinny.

"I'll help," he said. "What could I do?"

"Stone-age village," said Jinny. "It's only to be copied from this book. Thanks."

The essay was on Shylock. Jinny wrote three pages and then turned her attention to the French sentences. A quarter of an hour later she had finished.

"Super village," she said to Mike. "I'd better just touch it up a bit in case they guess I didn't do it." Taking her wax crayons, Jinny began to colour Mike's drawing.

Mike sat back on his heels watching enviously as his picture came to life under Jinny's hands. She added several hunting dogs, drew a herd of wild ponies looking down at the village from the hillside, two or three skin-clad people standing about the huts, then put a huge sun into the sky dominating the whole picture, its rays beating down on the village as they did in Egyptian pictures Jinny had seen.

"You didn't need me," said Mike.

"I did. It would have taken me ages to copy it correctly and really that's what Mrs. Crowther wants."

When her father had seen her homework, Jinny ran down to the stable and mixed a feed for Easter. She paused, wondering if she should go and see Shantih first.

"No," Jinny decided. "I'll see her last. Then I can spend all the time I've got left with her. Mr. MacKenzie first."

The farmer was sitting on the bench in front of his farm, his feet in their tacketty boots stuck straight out in front of him, his shirt sleeves rolled up, his waistcoat buttons undone, his cap pulled down over his nose and his short-stemmed blackened pipe held between his teeth. He didn't look up as Jinny approached.

Jinny sat down beside him, waiting for him to speak to her. Mr. MacKenzie puffed away, ignoring Jinny.

"You've seen Easter?" asked Jinny at last, forced into speech.

"Aye, if that's the name you've given to that skinful of bones that's eating my grass. Grass I was keeping for the heifers I'm buying from Charlie Moss next month. Aye, I've seen her."

"Oh no!" gasped Jinny. She had never once imagined that there might be anything special about the field by the bothy. It had just looked to Jinny like any other grass, only longer and sweeter.

"I never thought it was special grass!"

"You'd have been doing better to have been asking my permission first, before you went putting a beast like yon on my land."

Mr. MacKenzie never looked at Jinny; he went on staring straight ahead and smoking his pipe so that Jinny knew he was really annoyed.

"I didn't mean to do any harm."

"Oh, I'm sure of that. Here and there like a flea in a colander, minding other peoples' businesses, that's the style of you and, 'So sorry, Mr. MacKenzie,' when the damage has been done. 'I didn't know, Mr. MacKenzie.' 'I didn't mean it, Mr. MacKenzie,' " mocked the farmer in Jinny's voice.

Jinny stood up. There was obviously no point in wasting any more time. Mr. MacKenzie was umbraged and intended to stay that way.

"I'll take her down to Shantih's field," Jinny said.

"Och, be leaving the poor thing where she is now. Keziah has taken the bit fancy to her. Though next time," warned Mr. MacKenzie, taking the pipe out of his mouth and pointing it at Jinny, "be asking my permission first."

"I will," said Jinny. "Don't worry."

Jinny left the farmyard and began to climb up to the bothy. She felt so tired that she thought she could have lain down in the bracken and slept. It was an effort to walk, to lift one leaden foot and place it down in front of the other; the bucket of food was a dead weight in her hand.

Events of the past day and night flickered through Jinny's mind as she plodded on. Brenda's gaudy face became Miss Lorimer's prim disapproval; Mr. MacKenzie's fixed basilisk gaze became the Headmaster's bald authority; Shantih became as poor as Easter, the flesh withering from her, great hollows sunk above her eyes, the beauty of her proud bearing and arrogant breeding fallen into the gaunt frame of Don Quixoté's mare Rosinante. Her lameness became Easter's broken, shuffling gait. Jinny's mother and father watched, and Petra's starling voice asked endless questions that Jinny couldn't answer. The man in the white coat at the Vet College said that the X-ray showed navicular.

Jinny rounded a corner of the track and the bothy came into sight. In the doorway sat a wise woman; her long grey hair fell to her shoulders, her black robes covered her feet, and a cloak patterned with mystic symbols was brilliant about her. A white beast crouched at her side, its head resting on her knee. Unicorn or hart or mare. Jinny couldn't tell. She stopped, stared, held by the vision.

"It's yourself has been the long time coming," said Keziah.

Blinking, shaking her head, Jinny walked towards the old tinker woman and the white pony lying beside her. Keziah's hair was loose, her rusty black clothes grew on her and round her shoulders was a brightly-patterned shawl.

94

"I thought . . ." began Jinny vaguely.

"Be sitting you down," said Keziah, pointing to a wooden stool.

Thankfully, Jinny collapsed on to the stool. "Do you know, I thought . . ."

Easter, disturbed by Jinny's arrival, got to her feet and stood looking out over the moorland.

"Tam was telling me it was yourself saved the pony."

"Well, Brenda really," said Jinny, standing up again and holding out the feed to Easter. "Brenda said I could have her. I've to pay for her before the end of the month. If I hadn't saved her, she would have been dead by now."

For a moment, Jinny thought about the other horses from the riding school who would have been loaded into the slaughterer's float that morning, but there was nothing she could have done for them. She had done all she could. She had saved Easter.

"It was the right thing to do," said Keziah gently.

At her words, Jinny felt the turmoil inside her head begin to settle and grow calm so that she could reach the deep, still place within herself, and Keziah's voice was the voice of this stillness. It had been the right thing to do.

When Easter had finished her feed she began to graze, and Jinny sat down again sharing the evening silence with Keziah, gazing down over the reach of moorland to where the sea lipped and clipped in a quicksilver quiescence. Somehow it was as if she had always known Keziah, or had found her after searching for her all her life. She was someone who understood how it was for Jinny. Ken did in a way, but he was still searching himself. Keziah had a peace about her. She knew and rested in the knowing. If she only would, she could tell Jinny all she wanted to know.

"It's your family will be all away on Saturday?" Keziah asked.

Jinny looked up, startled back into present things.

"Why, yes," she said, wondering why Keziah should care.

"But it's yourself will be there?"

"I'm not going with them. I can't stand that Belinda Wright. I'm staying at home."

Keziah nodded as if it mattered to her, then Maggie and Tam, carrying bags of shopping, came round the track.

There was chatter and fussing when Maggie saw Keziah still sitting in the doorway. Bustling, she helped Keziah into the bothy, demanding to know why Jinny hadn't had the sense to put peat on the fire.

"Was Mr. MacKenzie mad when he saw Easter in his field?" Jinny asked Tam.

"Aye. Said he'd be dealing with you when he saw you."

"He's seen me. Still, he said she could stay."

"There'll be no trouble with her now," said Tam. "It's herself that has taken to the pony. I'll keep the eye on her, be seeing that she's not eating too much of the rich grass. I'll be bringing her out here to graze."

With her hand on Easter's neck, Jinny walked beside her back to the field, talking to her, feeding her bits of bread.

"She can't be," Jinny told herself. "It really is my imagination this time." For to Jinny's loving eye, Easter looked a bit better already. Her eyes were brighter, her ears flickered to the sound of Jinny's voice, and when she left Easter in the field and went down to Shantih, Jinny looked back and saw Easter with her head down grazing steadily.

"You've to go to the Vet College," she told Shantih, standing still while the Arab blew over her hair. "Not this Saturday but next. It's more or less all fixed up. Oh, why are you lame? Why can't you get better?"

Jinny stood gazing into the greying evening. She did not know how she could ever bear to take Shantih to the Vet College knowing that her lameness might be incurable. Leading her into Danny Sargent's float, knowing where they were taking her, what they would do to her—and Shantih not knowing.

"Oh, please, please Shantih, couldn't you get better then we won't need to go?" Jinny pleaded uselessly.

Jinny went straight to the phone when she got into the house. She stood staring down at its black toad waiting, then she drew in a deep breath, grasped the receiver and dialled the vet's number.

Jim Rae was sharp and businesslike. The Manders would pay for half of the petrol, and she was to mention to her father that a bottle left in the float for Danny would be acceptable.

"There's absolutely nothing else we could try?" Jinny asked.

"Brisk up," said the vet. "You're only taking her for an X-ray, not an execution. Be ready seven o'clock, a week this Saturday."

"Yes," said Jinny and almost, almost she didn't ask.

"Right," said the vet, ready to put the phone down.

"It could be navicular, couldn't it?" Jinny demanded, her voice high-pitched and anxious, pleading with the vet to say no, of course it couldn't, not to be so silly.

There was a moment's pause.

"Whatever put that into your head?"

"But it could be, couldn't it?"

"We can't rule out the possibility, but don't upset yourself about it. Wait until we see what the X-ray shows. We'll cross that bridge if we come to it."

Jinny went upstairs to her room. She sat on her bed, staring down the garden to the horses' field. Bramble grazed steadily, walking smoothly, but Shantih stood still, stretching her neck to reach as much grass as she could without moving, then she stumbled forward and stood still to graze again.

"You must want them to find out what's wrong with her. She can't go on like this," Jinny told herself.

"No!" Jinny said aloud. "No!" She could not bear the thought of taking Shantih to the Vet College that would smell the same as Inverburgh Hospital; could not bear the thought of the suave, self-assured face above the white coat telling her that it was a fractured bone, that it was navicular.

Jinny jumped up, sweeping the terror out of her head. She swung through to the other half of her room, laid out paper, sharpened a pencil and sat down to draw pictures for Nell Storr, pictures that would sell for enough money to pay for Easter.

But the pictures refused to come. The pencil in Jinny's hand was a clumsy piece of dead wood not a living extension of her being, the way it usually was. It was no good, she could not draw anything tonight. There was no magic.

At last Jinny gave up trying.

"Are you in?" called her mother's voice.

"I'm in," replied Jinny. "And getting ready for bed."

"Good," said Mrs. Manders. "Sleep well."

Jinny got up and went to stand in front of the Red Horse.

"Cure Shantih's lameness," she begged. "Let her be fit again. Make her fit to gallop and jump. Let me find out what's wrong with her foot before I need to take her to the Vet College."

The mural of the Red Horse was without power. Jinny stretched out her hand towards it, ran her fingers over the arched line of its neck, the bulk of its chest, its plunging legs and blocked hooves. With her forefinger Jinny traced the outline of its yellow eyes and trumpeting nostrils. But it was only a lifeless painting, a crude drawing with its paint flaking away in places.

If Jinny had stood there all night it would have made no difference. She turned away and, undressing, got ready for bed. She pulled the clothes over her head and buried her face in the pillow. There were too many challenges in Jinny's life for her to start and think about them tonight.

Just before she slept, the pressure of the Red Horse, as it had once been when it had haunted Jinny's dreams, strayed into the edge of her consciousness. It was like the sun that Jinny had drawn above Mike's stone-age village; the rays from the Horse reached out encircling Keziah and Easter, Jinny and Shantih. It stayed, brilliantly waiting, for them to approach it. Waited, knowing that they would come.

CHAPTER TEN

The noise of Petra having a bath woke Jinny on Saturday morning. She sat up in bed, checked automatically that Shantih and Bramble were in their field, then thought how satisfactory it was that she wasn't going to have to go into Inverburgh with her family and spend the day with Belinda Wright. Positive action obviously paid off. Jinny noted the fact for future use. If she had said weakly that she really didn't want to meet the Wrights again, never having been at all fond of Belinda when they had been in the same class in their Stopton school, and would her family mind if she stayed at Finmory and didn't meet them, they would probably have persuaded her to go with them. A strong "No" had made everything quite definite from the start.

Before breakfast, Jinny went down to see Shantih and Bramble.

"You might have been going to the Vet College today," Jinny told Shantih, shivering suddenly at the thought. "At least the Wrights have done some good going home through Inverburgh. They've put that off for a week."

Shantih listened with alert ears to Jinny's voice.

"You'd give anything to be sound again, wouldn't you?" Jinny murmured. "So we could go for a ride again." And Jinny thought of all the rides they had shared—quiet rides along the beach in the early morning, rides over the moors, the race to the standing stones when Shantih had jumped the waterfall.

"What will I do? What will I do if it is navicular? If it is a fractured bone? I couldn't bear to let them shoot you. Couldn't. Not ever. Not ever. Please God, no. No. They'll tell me to be sensible about it. Tell me it's the only thing."

Shantih, sensing Jinny's distress, gazed at her through solemn eyes. Listening to her. Trying to understand.

For a brief moment, Jinny laid her face against Shantih's neck.

"It would have been today," she murmured. "If Dad

99

hadn't thought I was going with them to see the Wrights, I'd have known by tonight."

A bit of Jinny knew that she couldn't go on like this. In the end, Shantih would have to go to the Vet College, Jinny would have to know, but just now she couldn't face up to it. She pushed it out of her mind, spun round away from Shantih and ran back to the house.

Her family were having an early breakfast, all looking smart and unlike their usual Saturday morning selves.

"It would have been so much nicer if you'd been coming with us," said her mother, as Jinny sat down and spooned muesli from the big bowl on to her own plate. "Mrs. Wright will think it very odd."

"She thinks I'm odd no matter what I do," stated Jinny.

"I'm dying to see Susan again," said Petra, making sure that nobody thought she was odd.

"Surprise, surprise," mocked Jinny.

"I don't see why I have to go when you're letting Jinny stay at home," said Mike. "I don't want to go a bit. It's not fair, dragging me into Inverburgh."

"Silence," ordered Mr. Manders. "Eat."

"Jinny would have been far better coming with us," insisted Petra. "All you'll do is moon about over Shantih. As if that's doing her any good. What you should be doing is getting her X-rayed as soon as possible. That's what would do her some good. Find out why she is lame."

"Shut up," said Jinny, scowling at her sister. Never in a million years would Petra understand why Jinny couldn't bear the thought of taking Shantih to the Vet College. Petra's world was crisp and smart, held together by time tables and examinations successfully passed. It was black and white and Petra intended to keep it that way.

"A good chance for you to get on with your homework," said Mr. Manders. "I'll look at it tomorrow morning and if it's not done properly you're not going out until it is."

"Say nothing," Jinny told herself. "Another hour and they'll all have gone," and she bit her tongue between her teeth.

It was after ten before Mr. Manders drove out of Finmory drive. Jinny stood on the steps waving, Kelly at her side, for Ken had gone too, taking the chance of a lift to see Nell.

100

Jinny waited until she knew they would all be well past Mr. MacKenzie's, then she danced through the house, swinging her arms, stamping her feet, in and out through every room, making the house her own.

"First," thought Jinny, when she eventually threw herself flat on the kitchen floor in utter exhaustion, "I'm going to mix a feed for Easter, then bring her down here and try to groom her a bit. Then I shall do some pictures for Nell."

Jinny went down to the stables and mixed oats, nuts and two handfuls of the mixture into a bucket. She had brought apples and carrots from the house and she cut these into long strips, added them to the feed, then stirred it round with her hands.

"Better damp it," Jinny thought, going outside to where a rain barrel stood by the stable door. A movement on the hillside caught her eye and instantly, calling Kelly to heel, Jinny dodged back into the stable.

"Knew there was something going on," she thought, as she crouched down by the stable window and peered up the hill. "This is why Keziah wanted everyone out of Finmory."

Down from the hill came Easter being led by Tam. Keziah, supported by Maggie, was sitting sideways on her back.

"What on earth can she be doing," Jinny wondered, as she watched the shabby procession descending from the hill. Maggie's days in the bothy had changed her plastic, new-housing-estate image back into Maggie of the tinker days. A man's anorak covered a rough dress, she wore heavy wellingtons, and her hair was drawn back into a knot at the nape of her neck. Keziah was slumped almost double over Easter's neck. In her black cowl of shawl and plaid, she looked like a shelled woman, hunched against fate, her gnarled face indomitable. Easter was worn out, pathetic, and Tam was sleekit, furtive. Jinny saw them through Miss Tuke's eyes. They were tinkers, not to be trusted, coming to steal.

At Jinny's feet, Kelly snarled, his hackles rising. Jinny silenced him. Crouching down, she gripped his collar, told him to be quiet, but the dog growled in his throat, wrinkling his muzzle over white teeth.

"It's all right," said Jinny. "You know them. It's OK."

She looked up out of the window again. Keziah was tall and stately, the robes she wore about her shoulders trailed to the ground. She rode a white mare, proud-stepping with eye imperial and cascading mane and tail. A hand-maiden walked by her side, and a page boy walked at the head of her palfrey. All the fairy-tales Jinny had ever read, all the illustrations she had ever seen of queens upon white horses, or wise women, of elfin lands, took hands and danced in Jinny's sight. She watched spellbound.

For a minute they dropped out of sight as the track looped downhill and when they reappeared the spell was broken. They appeared tinkers and an old pony again.

Tam led Easter up to Finmory's back door. Maggie helped Keziah down from Easter then supported her into Finmory. Minutes later, Maggie came out alone and she and Tam took Easter back up the hill out of Jinny's sight.

"Take the food to Easter," Jinny told herself. "Go up the hill to Maggie and Tam. Ask them what Keziah is doing." But she put the bucket of food down on the stable floor and went towards the house, Kelly padding at her side. She stood outside the back door, the familiar door-handle smooth and comforting in her hand. Then she turned it and went in.

Jinny walked up the wide curving staircase and the empty house seemed to vibrate to a strange low keening. The chant, the mouth music, the vibration, grew stronger as Jinny walked slowly along the corridor and stopped at the stairs that climbed up to her own room. The chanting was coming from there.

Jinny climbed the steps, opened her door, walked in and under the archway. Her table and chair had been pulled towards the window. Keziah knelt on the floor in front of the Red Horse. Smoke rose from a stone bowl, sweet-smelling herbs that somewhere in a lost dream Jinny had smelt before. The chanting of the old woman filled the room, changed it.

Jinny stood uncertainly until Keziah turned to her and gestured her forward.

At Keziah's side were seven earthenware pots each containing a different colour of paint, a jar of water and two paintbrushes. She handed the pot of red paint and the larger of the two paintbrushes to Jinny.

Jinny opened her mouth to speak, to ask Keziah what she

was doing, what she wanted her to do, but words were out of Jinny's reach. Her mind couldn't get back to where speech was possible.

Now there was only the vibration of Keziah's chanting.

Jinny stood in front of the Horse, felt the chanting resonate through her body, lift her being clear from her mind. She dipped the brush into the red paint and, with a sure, steady stroke, began to repaint the Red Horse; the body glowing red; mane, tail, hooves, black; the leaves green, blue and purple ; the fleshy blossoms white. Jinny re-created the Horse. She knew she was doing it, yet it was not herself, her everyday self, but some vital force that flowed through her. Last of all, Jinny painted in the Horse's yellow eyes.

Keziah rose up from the floor. Taking the other paint-brush, she dipped it into the red paint, touched pupils into the yellow eyes, and the Red Horse could see again. The room was filled with its presence. Keziah's chant grew louder, more urgent. Jinny crouched down, shielding her face until the chanting faded into a silence as sweet as the taste of true water. Jinny opened her eyes.

The freshly-painted mural was luminous and somehow, in the light that came from the Horse, Jinny could see Shantih galloping, free in her element, made whole again.

"Shantih, Shantih," Jinny cried into the silence. But the vision had gone. There was only Keziah lying amongst the shrouds of her black clothes, her eyes closed, her weathered skin stretched tight over her eagle-nose, high cheekbones and ridged jawbone. The pots of paint were empty, the brushes and the water soiled, the herbs burned out.

Jinny sat up, swung her hair back from her face, shaking her head to clear her mind, to come back into herself again. The power that had possessed her had gone. Jinny couldn't even begin to understand what it was. Something to do with the mystery of the Red Horse, Jinny's own red hair and Shantih, glowing chestnut—all fire things, flaunting, magic. And somehow it was close to the way Jinny felt when one of her paintings was going so right that not Jinny but something else was painting it.

She sat beside Keziah, supporting the old woman until she was sitting, leaning against Jinny. There was no substance to her body, brittle bones under slack skin, as if only her clothes held her together. Gradually Keziah opened her eyes.

"Are you all right?" Jinny asked anxiously, as Keziah turned her face to the Horse.

"You did well," she said. "It is the work well done before I go."

Jinny helped her to her feet. For a long moment the old woman stood before the Horse, then she turned and without looking back made her slow way through the arch and out of the door.

"I'll not be seeing it again with these eyes," she said, as Jinny helped her down the stairs. "I will not be staying long in this body now."

All her mother's easy reassurances sprang to Jinny's lips, but she couldn't say them. They would be too false. Keziah was dying. There was no need for pretence.

When at last they reached the kitchen, Jinny helped Keziah into a chair then busied herself making tea. Keziah sat as still as Tam.

"I've made it really sweet for you," said Jinny. "Could you eat anything? There's scones or biscuits."

Keziah took a biscuit and drank the sugary tea without speaking. When she had finished, she placed the mug firmly on the table in front of her.

"If you bring the Arab to me," she said, "I will be finding out for you the reason for her lameness."

"You what?" demanded Jinny.

"Bring her to me," repeated Keziah.

"But how could you tell what's wrong with Shantih? How would you know when there's nothing to see. She's just lame . . ." Jinny's words trailed into silence. Keziah sat as if Jinny hadn't spoken.

Jinny stared at her unbelievingly. How could Keziah know what was wrong with Shantih? An old tinker woman couldn't find out why she was lame when the vet had failed. Or could she? Could she know?

"I'll bring her," said Jinny and, hair bannering behind her, she wheeled round out of the kitchen and down to Shantih's field.

CHAPTER ELEVEN

Jinny fumbled the halter on to Shantih, led her through the gate, and slowly, limping and stumbling, Shantih followed Jinny up to the house. At the back door Jinny stopped. She pushed the door open and called into the kitchen that Shantih was there.

"Be bringing her in," replied Keziah.

"But I can't," shouted Jinny. "My mum would have a thousand canaries—a horse in her kitchen!"

"Bring her in to me."

Shantih stepped into the kitchen at Jinny's side, her neck arched, eyes goggling, nostrils flared. She was tight with panic, ready to leap away, shying from the strange objects that surrounded her, the sense of a prison, a cage.

Keziah spoke in a low, lilting voice, crooning and gentle, and Jinny felt the tenseness leave Shantih as she stretched her neck and blew over Keziah. The old woman's stiffened hands moved over Shantih's head and neck, her voice murmuring as she did so.

Shantih lowered her head on to Keziah's shoulder, and the old woman laid her face against the Arab's flat cheekbone. Lifting her arms, Keziah laid a hand on either side of Shantih's neck. She spoke gently, soothing Shantih, breathing peace and love into her.

At last Keziah straightened up and, lifting Shantih's lame leg, held the foot in both her hands. Jinny watched as Shantih stood perfectly still, allowing Keziah to examine her foot, making no attempt to draw it back from Keziah's control as the old woman carefully examined the sole and frog of Shantih's foot.

As Jinny stood holding Shantih she felt lost in a sense of total unreality. All the things that told her who she was, kept her safely linked to her pattern of everyday life, seemed to have fallen away leaving only the repainting of the Red Horse vivid in her mind. And now, the unreality of Shantih being in their kitchen, standing so peacefully while Keziah examined her foot; Shantih, who normally would have reared and plunged away if Jinny had suggested she should come into the house.

Keziah's eyes closed. She sat motionless, her hands cradling Shantih's hoof, and still Shantih stood without the least movement.

"In a way," Jinny thought suddenly, "It is the same as if I'd taken her to the Vet College. When Keziah tells me what's wrong it will be the same as the vet in the white coat confirming a fractured bone or navicular. I'll know any minute now. If Keziah says she can't be cured, that's it, final."

Ever since the moment when Shantih had laid her head on Keziah's shoulder and the old woman had bent her head to meet the Arab, Jinny had known that Keziah's power that had held her while she repainted the Horse, now bound Shantih in its spell. More surely than any veterinary diagnosis, Keziah would know what was causing Shantih's lameness.

At last Keziah's eyes opened. She freed Shantih's foot and Shantih placed it back precisely on to the kitchen floor. Keziah laid her hand on Shantih's shoulder, lowered her face for a last moment of communion with the horse, then sank back in her chair.

Jinny couldn't speak to ask what she was desperate, yet terrified, to discover. She could only wait.

"Do not be distressing yourself," said Keziah. "It is a poison deep in her foot. I felt something sharp—a piercing in her foot."

"Not navicular? Not a fractured bone?" cried Jinny.

"There is no disease," stated Keziah. "It is an injury. Not a broken bone for I was feeling the poison. Be taking her back to her field and come yourself to the bothy, and I will find the herbs to be drawing the poison out of her."

"You're all right, you're all right," Jinny cried, as she led Shantih back to her field. "It's not navicular. You'll be all right. I'll be able to ride you again. She can cure you. You don't need to go to the Vet College. Oh, Shantih, Shantih."

Jinny let Shantih go and stood watching her as she made her slow way across to Bramble. "Thank you. Thank you," said Jinny aloud. She stood for a long moment, freed from the terror of the unspeakable thought that Shantih might have had an incurable lameness, that she might never have been able to ride her again.

They brought Easter down to Finmory, and Maggie and Jinny helped Keziah up on to her back. Jinny could see that Maggie was concerned for Keziah and yet she said nothing, no reproaches or selfish fussing. The work that had brought Keziah to the bothy had been done.

When at last they reached the bothy, they had to carry Keziah inside and lay her on the couch. She sank back, her breath harsh, her face toned in yellows and greens, the great shadows around her eyes and nostrils, black purple. Jinny was appalled by the change. It seemed to have happened so suddenly.

Before she fell into a heavy sleep, Keziah told Tam to bring her bag to her and, from the black sack, Keziah drew out crumpled packets of dried herbs. She chose three of them, gave them to Jinny and told Tam the names of the herbs he would find growing on the moor.

"Be waiting here and Tam will bring them to you," Keziah told Jinny, her voice weak, used up, a harsh wrack of sound that Jinny could hardly hear as she told her how to make a poultice, apply it to the sole of Shantih's foot, binding it tightly into the frog and leaving it in position for a week.

"Do not be touching it for seven days," she warned. "By then it will have drawn the evil from her foot."

By the time Tam came back with the plants Keziah had told him to collect, Keziah was asleep. Maggie put the dried herbs and the ones Tam had brought, into the saucepan, added water and put the pan on the peat fire.

"They'll be ready by the afternoon," she told Jinny. "Be coming back then."

When Jinny went back there was no sign of Maggie or Tam. Keziah was lying as she had been when Jinny had left, closed into a heavy sleep. The pot of herbs simmered on the fire.

"Better wait till they get back," Jinny decided, and she took the feed she had brought for Easter out to where the pony was lying dozing in the shade.

When Jinny approached her, Easter got stiffly to her feet, shook herself and stepped towards Jinny, her eyes bright, her nostrils wiffling a welcome.

"Dear pony," said Jinny, setting the bucket of feed on the ground and watching as Easter buried her head in it, eager for the oats.

When Easter had finished feeding, Jinny put on the halter that she kept by the field gate and, using the dandy-brush that she had brought up with her from Finmory, began to groom the pony. Clouds of white hairs flew up from Easter's harsh coat.

"Bet it's years since anyone groomed you properly," Jinny told the pony. "You'll feel a lot better when I've finished."

As Jinny worked, happiness sparked electric through her. Shantih didn't have navicular, wouldn't have to go for an X-ray; in a week she would be sound and Jinny would be riding her again. Soon Easter would be coming down to the Finmory field; already she was coming alive again, beginning to be herself. Once she was at Finmory, Jinny would get her feet attended to and ask the vet to have a look at her.

Jinny brushed out her mane, patiently teasing out the tangles, sweeping it from one side of her neck to the other until it fell in a silver sheen almost as silken as Shantih's. After a few attempts to do something with the corded mat of Easter's tail, Jinny gave up.

"That can wait for another day," she said and, taking off Easter's halter, she sat down on the grass. The pony waited beside her.

"Where did you come from?" Jinny wondered, reaching up to scratch Easter's face. "To be here today to carry Keziah down to the Red Horse. When you were a show pony all poshed up with rosettes, did you know then that you would be here today? When was then? How were you young then and old now? What changes us?"

Jinny lay flat on the grass staring up at the sky, conscious of Easter beside her; of Keziah asleep in the bothy knowing that she was soon to die and seeming not to mind, not trying to cling on to breathing but letting it happen; of her family somewhere in Inverburgh being polite and plastic with the Wrights; and of Shantih who, by this time next week, would be sound again. And again Jinny felt the presence of Easter as clearly as she had done when she had seen her being ridden through the Inverburgh streets. As if the pony communicated with her through a sense that Jinny hardly knew she possessed, but that this time the sharing was of contentment and peace.

It was late afternoon before Tam and Maggie came back. Several times Jinny had looked in to the bothy to check that Keziah was still asleep and the herbs were still bubbling in the pot.

"We were sending the word," said Maggie. "It'll not be long now. Only the few days."

Jinny shivered, asked quickly if the poultice would be ready yet. When she went in with Maggie and Tam, Jinny kept close beside them, but Keziah lay without moving, sleeping deeply.

Maggie gave Jinny the pot to take down with her.

"Be binding it tight now," she cautioned. "And mind the old one's words—not to be touching it for the seven days."

To Jinny's delight, Ken was back home. She told him what had happened.

"You repainted the Horse?" said Ken, his eyes lighting. "Whee! Really nice. Can I see it?"

Jinny looked down at the soggy mess of herbs in Maggie's pot.

"Help me do Shantih's foot first," she said.

"Right," said Ken, "what do we need?"

"Cotton wool, bit of that green oilskin stuff that Mum used for Mike's arm, bandage—that's in the stable—and a sack. Oh, and scissors and Elastoplast."

"I'll get the things from the house," said Ken.

"I'll bring Shantih into her box. Be best to do her foot there. We can tie her up."

When Jinny led Shantih into her box, Ken had already assembled the things they needed to hold the poultice of herbs in place against the sole of Shantih's foot.

Even with Ken's calming influence, getting the poultice in place on Shantih's foot wasn't easy. First Jinny washed Shantih's hoof, then packed the green, strong-smelling mess of herbs into the sole of her foot. She laid a thick covering of cotton wool over the sole, held this in place with strips of Elastoplast, then put a covering of the green oiled skin over it. With Ken's help, she cut sacking into a rough boot shape and put the whole hoof into the sacking shoe. But even when she had bandaged it securely, it did not look as if it would stay in place for one day, let alone seven.

"Whoa lass, whoa Shantih," crooned Jinny, soothing the restless Arab.

"It won't do," said Ken. "She'll have it off in an hour."

Despondently Jinny agreed, but she couldn't think of any other way of keeping the poultice on.

"She needs a proper shoe," said Ken. "Know any horse shoe shops?"

"Oh, dozens," said Jinny. "There's two in Glenbost."

"Nip down and buy . . ."

"But I do know where I can get one," interrupted Jinny, remembering suddenly the leather poultice boots for horses that stood in a row on one of the shelves in Mr. MacKenzie's back porch. "If he'll lend me one, I'll get one at the farm."

Jinny left Ken holding Shantih while she raced down to Mr. MacKenzie's trying to think of the best way to ask for a loan of one of the boots. She hadn't seen Mr. MacKenzie since he had told her off for leaving Easter in his field. He might well refuse to lend her one of his poultice boots.

Luck was on Jinny's side. As she ran into the yard, one of Mr. MacKenzie's Shetlands, with a rope trailing from her neck, came bucketing out.

"Shouldn't be loose," thought Jinny, and flung herself at the pony, grabbing its rope, then its muzzle, as the Shetland, doing its very best rocking-horse imitation, struggled to escape.

Mr. MacKenzie, scarlet-faced, came stomping across the yard in hot pursuit.

"How many times," said Jinny, as Mr. MacKenzie pulled a halter on to the Shetland, "have I to tell you no to be leading a beast about on a wee bit rope? It's no safe."

"Aye," said Mr. MacKenzie. "It's quick you were there."

"Jet-set Jinny," replied Jinny, knowing it would be O.K. —Mr. MacKenzie would lend her a boot for Shantih.

When Mr. MacKenzie had returned the escapee Shetland to its stall, Jinny told him what she wanted.

"Och now, is that not an improvement, to be asking before you're taking?" said Mr. MacKenzie. He led Jinny round to the back porch and brought down two of the leather boots, knocking the spiders out of them before he handed them to her.

It's one of those two should be fitting her," he said.

"Thanks," said Jinny.

"It's honoured you were that Keziah was curing your horse. Her father, he was a whisperer. Could speak the healing words into a horse's ear. Some said it was Old Nick was putting the speech on his tongue, though my father aye said it was the herbs he used that did the healing. The gift passed on to Keziah, but she took against it and no money would make her use it. Only the tinkers' horses would she be treating, though it's the gentry themselves I've seen pleading at her."

"She whispered to Shantih."

"Aye."

One of the boots fitted Shantih's foot perfectly. Jinny buckled it securely into place. Leading Shantih back to the field, the Arab seemed more lame than ever with the clumsy boot on her foot.

"Only a week," Jinny assured her. "A week and you'll be sound again."

In the kitchen, Ken had made apple and carrot juice and cut slices of his home-baked bread, covering them with honey.

"Delish," said Jinny. "Haven't eaten since breakfast. Oh! Better phone the vet first."

"Vet?"

"To tell him I'll not need to take Shantih for the X-ray," Jinny called back, already on her way to the phone.

It was Mrs. Rae who answered, said she was glad to hear that Shantih was sound again, that Jim had been worried about her.

"Will be," said Jinny.

"Pardon?"

"Will be sound next weekend," said Jinny and, thanking her, put the phone down. It would have been too difficult trying to explain to Mrs. Rae.

When they had finished their snack, Jinny took Ken up to see the mural.

Ken stood in silent admiration in front of the Red Horse. The colours from Keziah's earthenware pots could not have been ordinary poster paint, or any other paint that Jinny knew of. They glowed from the wall as if light vibrated in them; they made the mural luminous.

"Whee!" exclaimed Ken at last, with a long drawn-out breath. "And you painted it?"

"In a way," said Jinny uncertainly. "In a way it was Keziah. I don't know how it did it. Not really. I couldn't have painted it without Keziah."

"I'm taking Kelly down to the sea," invited Ken, when at last he turned away from the mural.

"Better do some homework," said Jinny, but she didn't. When Ken had gone, she took out paper and paints, spread them out on the floor and, sitting back on her heels, stared at the white paper. For Jinny, no experience was ever complete until she had drawn or painted it in some way.

First she painted the tinkers coming down the hillside. Tam crunched into his caddis shell of clothes, Maggie supporting an old bent woman who hardly had the strength to cling on to the worn-out pony. Then the vision she had had of them—Keziah, the wise woman on her pacing palfrey attended by a young girl and a page. But they weren't enough. The first was too ordinary, the second too romantic. Jinny held both paintings in her mind's eye, tried again, screwed it up and started again. At her third attempt, she got what she wanted. They were tinkers, and Easter was old, but being themselves they were also the vision. It was there in the angle of Keziah's neck, her hands, her cloak; in Tam and in Maggie, as the bright shadow of Easter's past was visible in her. When she had finished it, Jinny hardly glanced at it.

She put it up on her table and quickly did a pencil drawing of Shantih—Shantih sound again, the wind in her mane and tail.

Then Jinny took a piece of her precious pastel paper and with wax crayons drew the Red Horse, pressing the wax colour hard on to the black paper until it had a thick enamel quality.

Her family came back just as Jinny had finished it. For minutes Jinny listened to the banging of doors, their voices loud after the silence.

"Jinny, are you in?" called her mother.

"I'm in," Jinny replied, and went tearing down the staircase to tell them her day.

The phone rang before she reached the kitchen. Jinny doubled back into the hall and answered it. It was the vet.

112

"That's right," Jinny assured him. "No, I really don't need to take her to the Vet College now. She will be quite sound by next weekend. I'm perfectly sure."

Jinny held the receiver away from her ear so that she couldn't quite hear what the vet was saying, only knew when he had stopped talking.

"Fine," said Jinny into the phone. "Right then. Thank you," and she put the phone down.

"Belinda was most upset you weren't there," said Mrs. Manders.

"Who was it on the phone?" asked Mr. Manders.

"Susan had six-inch heels, at least," said Petra.

"The vet," said Jinny. "I'd phoned up earlier to tell him that Shantih wouldn't need to go to the Vet College."

"Not go for the X-ray?" interrupted Mike in amazement.

"But it was Mrs. Rae I got and that was Mr. Rae. Just checking, I suppose."

"You mean Shantih's sound?" demanded Mrs. Manders. "That's great. Tell us."

"Well, not exactly sound," said Jinny. "But she will be by next weekend." And Jinny told her family what had happened.

"You mean," said Petra, "just because that mad old tinker woman boiled up some plants into a poultice you think that's going to cure Shantih's lameness? You don't, Jinny? Even you couldn't be a naïve as that!"

Jinny stared in horror at her sister. Until Petra had spoken there had been utterly no doubt in Jinny's mind. To Jinny, Shantih was as good as cured. For seconds the shock of Petra's words was so great that Jinny could hardly believe what she had heard. How could anyone doubt that Shantih would be sound in seven days?

"Keziah knew what was wrong with her foot," said Jinny, "and she knew how to cure it. Shantih will be all right by next weekend."

"Well, we'll hope so," said her mother. "But I don't think you should have cancelled the arrangements with the vet."

"Better phone back and explain," suggested Mr. Manders. "Tell him you've discussed it with us and decided that Shantih had better go for the X-ray after all."

"No," said Jinny.

"Don't be so daft . . ." began Petra.

"I'm not daft and I'm not naïve, whatever that means," Jinny shouted. "Shantih is not going to the Vet College. She doesn't need to go. She will be sound by next weekend."

Jinny turned and dashed out of the room and up to her own bedroom. She looked down to where Shantih stood, resting her poulticed leg.

"They know nothing," muttered Jinny. "Nothing. By next week I'll be riding you again. Then they'll see that I'm not daft."

CHAPTER TWELVE

On Monday lunchtime Jinny took her paintings to Nell to see if she would buy them. She was making a discreet escape from school, for although it wasn't actually forbidden, pupils who took school dinners weren't encouraged to roam around Inverburgh at lunchtime, when Mr. Eccles spotted her.

"Jinny! Jinny Manders" he called.

Jinny turned, ready to defend her right to go to the shops if she wanted to.

"Glad I caught you," said her art teacher. "Have you a minute?"

Unwillingly Jinny admitted she had.

"Was having a word about you with the Headmaster this morning. Seems you're up to your neck in detentions and undone homework?"

Jinny said she supposed she was.

"Well, I told him that the art department had no complaints whatsoever. That your work is outstanding."

Jinny squirmed inwardly, as she always did when anyone praised her painting.

I'm not saying you won't have to apply yourself to your maths, but I thought I'd let you know you're not entirely unappreciated. Spent grim years myself struggling with science because my family thought it was the only thing for a boy. So I know what it's like."

Jinny twisted her hair not knowing where to look.

"O.K."

"Yes," said Jinny.

As she trotted through the crowded street, Mr. Eccles' words rang pleasantly in her mind. "Outstanding". "Not entirely unappreciated". Despite herself, she smiled as she hurried on to Nell's shop.

"I've got to get the money to Brenda before the month is up to pay for Easter," Jinny explained to Nell. "So could you put them somewhere where people will see them easily?"

Nell was looking intently at Jinny's pictures spread out on

her counter. There were the three of Maggie and Tam bringing Keziah down the hillside on Easter, three pencil drawings of Shantih, two of Kelly, and three other pastel drawings of Bramble and Shantih. Jinny had kept the one of the Red Horse for herself.

"I'll do better than that," said Nell. "I'll pay you in advance. Sale or return to begin with, but once a supplier is established I always buy the goods from them. Consider yourself established. Five pounds a picture—fifty-five pounds."

"But will you be able to sell them?" asked Jinny, feeling embarrassed by taking so much money from Nell.

"Picked up a rather nice selection of frames from a house clearance. I'll frame your pictures and make a filthy profit," Nell assured her. "Don't worry, I'm not giving money away."

Jinny took the money to the riding school on Tuesday after school.

Brenda was out with a ride, and Jinny had to hang about the yard waiting for her to return. Jinny wondered if Miss Tuke had been out yet to inspect things. There was no doubt about it, the place had been smartened up. The yard had been thoroughly swept and someone had started to repair the stabling. Jinny looked into the stalls and saw that the chestnut pony who was standing in had been thoroughly groomed and had hay in his manger. At the end of the row of stalls, instead of the rotten hay, there was a fresh load of sweet smelling bales and three brand-new, galvanized bins. As usual, Miss Tuke was effectively seeing to things.

It was almost half an hour before Brenda, accompanied by two men riding Sporty and Queenie, arrived back.

"How's tricks?" asked Brenda.

"I've got fifty-five pounds for you," said Jinny, holding out the money to Brenda. "So that's seventy-five altogether. I'm bound to get the other five in time, so she's quite safe."

Brenda took the money, flicking the notes through her fingers.

"Call it square," she said. "Your Miss Tuke got me a rise. Threatened to report Martin for not paying me a living wage. She's a one she is. Seventy-five will satisfy his lordship."

"Oh thanks. That's great."

"And how's Easter?"

"Super. She really is. Still in the field by the bothy, but I should think I'll take her down to the others next week and then I'll ask the vet to look at her."

"Get her wormed," said Brenda.

"Will do," said Jinny. "I made her a bran mash with treacle and oats and chopped apple on it. She smelt it and came cantering to the gate for it," Jinny's face was bright at the memory.

"I'll come and see her some time," said Brenda. "If it's O.K.?"

"'Course," said Jinny. "Do come. You can see Shantih. She's getting better too."

For a moment before Brenda turned away she smiled at Jinny, her mask drawn back, and, for a second, Jinny saw quite clearly the girl who had once shared her dreams.

Jinny raced for the bus and caught it by the skin of her teeth, but by the time she got home it was too late to go up to the bothy.

"I was up this morning," Mrs. Manders assured her. "Keziah's very weak. There's nothing you could do. You'll see her tomorrow night."

"But Easter—I should be feeding her."

"She was stuffing herself with grass. Shouldn't think she'd be thanking you for any other kind of food."

"Must go down and see Shantih, then," insisted Jinny. "I'll go now. I'll be very quick, then I'll come back and do my homework."

"Quarter of an hour," said her father.

"Oke," said Jinny, and went.

Shantih came hobbling to the gate, her hoof still safely inside its leather boot.

"Dear horse," said Jinny, rubbing Shantih's neck, straightening her mane and feeding her lumps of sugar. "How does your foot feel now? I can't see how it is now you're all cluttered up with that boot. Only another three days and I can take it off. Then you'll be sound again. Then we can go for rides again." To Jinny, not having Shantih to ride was almost like being lame herself. It seemed so long ago, the last time she had ridden Shantih on the moors. So long ago since she had galloped and jumped, felt Shantih winged beneath her as the moorland fell away under Shantih's flying hooves. "Soon you'll get out of this field, get down to the shore again," Jinny told her.

But Shantih was pushing at Jinny's pockets, pawing the ground, asking for more sugar-lumps.

It wasn't until Jinny was getting ready for bed that it suddenly struck her that Shantih had been standing on her lame leg and pawing the ground with her sound foot.

On Thursday night, Jinny only had English and French homework.

"Test my vocabulary," she said to Mike.

"I learnt it at lunchtime," she told him, when she'd got it all right.

"And that's my English essay," she said to her father, holding out her exercise book for his approval.

"Good," said Mr. Manders, when he had finished reading it. "Spelling original but A-plus for content."

"Am I free?"

"Miss Manders, you are absolutely free."

Jinny mixed a feed for Easter, putting in apples, sliced carrots, turnip, oats, maize and pony nuts. "Oat cocktail," she thought, setting off to the bothy.

Easter was grazing in the far corner of the field. When she saw Jinny she gave a shrill, trembling whinny and came eagerly to the gate.

"By the end of the summer you'll be quite fit again," Jinny thought optimistically, as she watched Easter wolfing down the feed. "Wonder if I could ride you? Or you could be a pack pony. We could go on a trek and you could carry the tent. Kelly could be a watch-dog."

Easter finished the feed, tipped the bucket over with her nose, then shied away from it's rattling menace. Jinny grinned, remembering how Easter had hardly noticed the oil drums and poles clattering about her legs.

For a while, Jinny stayed just watching Easter. At the end of her life, things were going right for her again. She would never leave Finmory. She would stay there with Shantih and Bramble until she died. The best had happened for her.

Reluctantly, Jinny turned away and walked across to the bothy. Inside, Keziah was lying on the couch, propped up with pillows, covered with blankets. Her eyes were closed and her breathing harsh. Maggie and two other tinker women Jinny hadn't seen before were sitting over the fire. They looked up uneasily, waiting for Jinny to go when she had just arrived.

"How is she?" Jinny asked awkwardly, feeling an intruder.

"Do not be disturbing her," cautioned Maggie. "She's sleeping easier now. Be leaving her in peace."

The gaunt face with its heavy grey hair was indrawn, not to be reached by Jinny's polite enquiries.

"I'll come back tomorrow night," said Jinny.

"Don't be upsetting yourself now," said Maggie kindly. "Keziah would not be wanting to stay here when she is ready to go."

Jinny went down to Mr. MacKenzie's to collect the milk. As she reached the yard, two rackety vans drove in, their doors opened and several tinkers unloaded themselves. One of the men spoke to Mr. MacKenzie, asking where Keziah Brodie was. The farmer pointed to the track. Children and dogs, women and men, came out of the vans and made their way up the track. Mr. MacKenzie stood watching them, smoking his pipe and spitting. Saying nothing.

"Not like him," thought Jinny. Normally the farmer would have been shouting after them, warning them to keep to the track, to shut gates and not to interfere with his stock. "Or chasing them off his land altogether," Jinny thought, and the strangeness of Mr. MacKenzie's behaviour shivered through Jinny like a cold finger laid on her spine. For the tinkers had come to be there when Keziah died.

"Aye, she was the bold one," said Mr. MacKenzie, giving Jinny the full can of milk. "The same Keziah Brodie. It's the sleepness nights I've spent tossing on my bed thinking of that one. Aye. So it is."

Jinny took the milk and hurried away. She didn't want to know.

As she came in sight of the horses' field, Shantih and Bramble were grazing. Jinny paused, changing the milk can to her other hand. Then she stood perfectly still, staring intently.

"If being sound was the worst thing in the world to happen to Shantih, the thing you most absolutely dreaded, so you would pretend she wasn't sound for as long as you could,

119

what would you think now?" Jinny asked herself. "You couldn't pretend she wasn't sound, could you? No matter how badly you wanted her to go on being lame, you'd have to admit she's not so lame."

Excitement welled up in Jinny, for Shantih, grazing beside Bramble, was moving easily, keeping pace with the Highland, taking her weight evenly on each leg as she walked.

"Not yet," Jinny warned herself, banking down the brimming joy that threatened to overflow inside her. "It's too soon. I can't be sure yet. Not till Saturday morning. Not until I take the poultice off."

On Friday afternoon, Mr. Manders was taking a load of pottery in to Nell and he had arranged to pick Jinny up outside her school.

"I'd have been quicker on the bus," Jinny thought irritably, as she waited, watching the hands of the school clock creep towards half-past four. "And I've so much to do."

It was almost a quarter to five before Mr. Manders appeared, and to Jinny's dismay there was someone sitting next to him in the car.

"Sorry," he said, opening a back door of the car for Jinny. "Got held up at Nell's."

Disgruntled, Jinny clambered in.

"I've been waiting for bloomin' ages," she grumbled, which was as far as she dared to go with a stranger in the car.

"Peter," said Mr. Manders, "this is Jinny, my daughter. Jinny, meet Mr. Drennan."

"How do you do?" said Jinny, wondering who Mr. Drennan was and why he was in their car. Most of all she was hoping that it didn't mean more wasted time before they got back home.

"Mr. Drennan was delivering some carvings to Nell, so I'm giving him a run back to his house," said Mr. Manders. "Save him hanging around waiting for a bus."

"Where to?" asked Jinny.

"Rashburn," said Mr. Manders.

Jinny sat back utterly defeated. It would be after seven before they got back to Finmory.

"Just when I wanted to be home as soon as possible," she thought. "Curses. Curses. Curses."

Mr. Drennan insisted that they should come in for coffee.

120

Coffee turned into beer for Mr. Manders and it was half-past eight before they were back at Finmory.

"Look at the time!" ranted Jinny. "I'll need to go up now to see Easter. I'd have caught the six o'clock bus if I'd known we were going to be as late as this."

"It wouldn't have made any difference what time you'd got home at, so calm yourself," said Mrs. Manders, who had come to the door when she heard the car. "Even if you'd been home at your usual time you couldn't have gone up to the bothy tonight."

"Why? I must go up and see Easter."

"Ken saw her this afternoon and she's fine. He took a feed up to her."

"But why can't I go up?"

"Too many tinkers up there," said Mrs. Manders. "No place for you tonight."

"Oh Mum, don't be so ridiculous . . ."

"Settled," said Mrs. Manders. "Even Mr. MacKenzie came round to tell me to be keeping the hems on you tonight."

"Final," said her father. "That's it." And Jinny knew there was no point in arguing.

"First thing tomorrow then," she promised herself.

Tomorrow. The seventh day. The day she could take off the poultice.

CHAPTER THIRTEEN

The buckles of the leather boot were so stiff that Jinny could hardly loosen them.

"Whoa, steady, steady horse," soothed Jinny, as Shantih, tied to the gate-post, pulled back against her halter rope, yet again snatching her hoof out of Jinny's grasp.

Jinny turned her sideways against the gate and patiently tried again. Kneeling in the dew-wet grass, she struggled to push the leather strap through the buckle. Time stood still. Jinny's world had shrunk to nothing but her concentration on the obdurate leather. In minutes the poultice would be off and Jinny would know.

At last Jinny managed to undo one buckle, which eased the tightness of the boot, and the other buckle opened easily. She took the leather boot off, untied the bandage, and the poultice with its paddings fell away from Shantih's foot. Lying on the mess of the poultice was a shard of stone about an inch long and sharp as a needle. It had been embedded in Shantih's foot and the poultice of herbs had drawn it out. Jinny wiped the sole of Shantih's foot clean, but there was no way of telling where her foot had been punctured.

Jinny untied Shantih, took off her halter and let her go free, her movements still slow and concentrated as if her actions were not linked by time, had no past, would have no future.

For a second the Arab stood poised, unmoving, and then she reared up, swung round on her quarters and charged full gallop round the field. Mane and tail fanned back by her speed, she charged round, a red-gold force. Her white hoofs beat a furious tattoo on the drum-skin of the earth; her speed sleeked the contours of her face into a precious, carven icon; the force of her quarters drove strength into her shoulders and chest. Round and round she went in power and glory. Shantih was sound again.

As Jinny watched, the weeks of misery dissolved, the dreaded threat of navicular or a fractured bone faded away.

For it had not happened, was not true. Shantih was sound. Jinny would be able to ride her again.

"Yarhoo, gaudeamus," yelled Jinny at the pitch of her lungs. She flung herself over the gate and went racing through the grey stillness to tell her family, to tell Keziah that Shantih was cured. No one was up in Finmory, but Jinny ran through the house shouting that Shantih was sound, that she had been right, that Keziah had cured her.

She slammed the back door shut behind herself and was about to run up the moors to the track that led to the bothy when suddenly she remembered that she didn't need to walk. She could ride. She could ride Shantih.

Jinny ran down to the stable, taking great leaps into the air, flinging her arms wide, shaking her hair for joy. She had to tell Keziah as soon as possible.

She grabbed Shantih's bridle from its hook, feeling its smooth leather familiar in her hand. She ran on down to the field where Shantih snatched mouthfuls of grass, then reared up, striking out with her forelegs before she bucked violently and tore round the field, flat out, the enclosure of the field turning her speed into a red-gold flame.

"Don't need to worry about whether I should ride her or not," Jinny thought. "She's sound O.K."

Jinny called her and Shantih flung up her head, stood for a moment taking in the bridle in Jinny's hand and then, knowing it meant a ride, came trotting to Jinny, her mane and tail bannering about her, high spring-stepping, bounding from a molten earth, her eyes lustrous with memory and expectation. Dour and stolid, Bramble grazed ignoring her.

Jinny slipped the reins over Shantih's head, slid the bit into her mouth and gently lifted the headpiece over her ears. She could hardly fasten the buckle of the throatlash her hands were shaking so much.

Jinny stood for a long moment, her hand laid flat on Shantih's neck, her being expanded with love. Never such a morning as this. Shantih was sound again.

Jinny gathered up her reins and sprang on to Shantih's back. Turning Shantih towards the moors, she touched her legs against the Arab's sides.

"We've got to tell Keziah that you're sound," Jinny said, as Shantih cantered on the spot, her tail kinked over her quarters, her neck and head high, her nostrils trumpeted into blood pits.

Jinny felt her drop behind the bit, her weight sink back on her hindlegs as she reared, struck out with her forefeet, then with an enormous bound was galloping up the track to the moor.

Shantih was all captured things flying free, was spirit loosened from flesh, was bird again in her own element. Jinny circled her once in a wide sweep over the open land then she turned her back to the path that lead to the bothy. In a way, Keziah already knew that Shantih would be sound, but Jinny wanted to see her again, to tell Keziah and to thank her.

As they reached the bothy, its air of stillness, of indrawn waiting, reached out to Jinny, striking cold against her jubilation. She dropped to a walk, remembering in a rush that there would be other tinkers there, not only Tam and Maggie and, with a chill tightening of her stomach, that Keziah was dying. But still her exultation carried Jinny on. She had to tell Keziah.

The door of the bothy was almost closed. Slipping down from Shantih, Jinny pushed it open. She had to let Keziah know that Shantih was cured.

The darkened room seemed crowded with tinkers standing about the couch, sitting on the floor. The only sound was the rasp of Keziah's breath as her lungs pushed out the unwanted air. Her eyes were closed. There was no flesh on her face, only her bones straining against the taut skin. Keziah was dying.

Jinny stood, clutching the buckle of Shantih's reins in her hand, desperate to escape but unable to move. Maggie came from Keziah's side and put her hand on Jinny's arm to take her out. At the disturbance, Keziah's eyes opened. It seemed to Jinny that they looked straight at her, and from somewhere beyond her eyes Keziah acknowledged her, knew that Shantih was cured.

Maggie steered Jinny out of the bothy.

"Be off home with you," she said. "There's no place for you here."

Tears running down her face, Jinny turned away. Leading Shantih, she walked round to the bothy field. Easter was standing four-square, her bony head stretched out towards the bothy, her ears sharp. She was so intent on what held her there that she seemed oblivious of Jinny's presence, did not even turn her head or flick an ear at Shantih but stood statue-still, gazing wistfully towards the bothy window.

Jinny waited by the field, arms folded along the top bar of the gate, her chin resting on them, Shantih's reins looped over her arm. Shantih, too, seemed caught in this spell of silence; her exuberance forgotten, she stood patiently waiting.

The sun brought back colour into the bleak moorland, to the mountains, to the dazzling rim of the sea. Still Jinny waited, unmoving. She did not understand death, its strangeness, its totality; that when someone died you would never see them again. When Jinny had been painting the Red Horse, Keziah had seemed like a part of herself. As if it was Keziah who had painted the Horse through Jinny and now . . .

Easter gave a sudden whinny and from the bothy came an indrawn shadow of sound, growing from it a high-pitched searing grief as the tinkers' keening mourned Keziah's death.

Now, even if Jinny were to search the whole world, over and over again, she would never find Keziah; never see her or hear her speak, not ever again. She was dead. Jinny stared out numbly across the moors, for it was not only Keziah who was dead, not some strange, special thing that had happened to her alone. This dying was a common thing, it happened to everything that lived; some day all her family would die, Jinny would die and even Shantih.

Jinny laid her arm over Shantih's withers, felt the strong, comforting presence of her horse close beside her.

Easter came slowly towards them. She reached out her head and breathed over Jinny's tear-stained face, exchanged curious questioning breath with Shantih, then stood waiting.

"Keziah's dead," said Jinny bleakly. "She's gone. No more. Dead."

Shantih rested her head on Jinny's shoulder, and Easter gazed at Jinny through eyes as wise as Keziah's had been. It was as if they understood more about death than Jinny could ever understand; that they knew death and life to be part of the same weaving, not in the easy way that humans used these words to cover over their fears, but deep in the very centre of their being. All their living was a part of this acceptance and they searched for a way to share this wisdom with Jinny.

Tam came out of the bothy, hesitated, looking about him. Seeing Jinny, he came towards her holding out a box.

"What is it?" Jinny asked, rubbing her arm across her face.

"For you," he said. "From Keziah."

Jinny opened the box. Inside were the seven earthenware pots of paint, each one refilled, carefully sealed, and the two paintbrushes and the stone bowl in which Keziah had burned the herbs while Jinny had painted the Red Horse.

"I'll keep them," she promised. "I'll put them in a safe place."

Tam nodded. "I'm away then," he said.

"Where will you go now?" Jinny asked.

"When we've buried the old one we'll be moving on."

"But where to?"

Tam shrugged.

"Don't you mind?" questioned Jinny. "Don't you mind that Keziah's dead?"

"She was ready to go," said Tam. His pinched face showed no sign of grief. "She died with her own folk. That's what she wanted."

And Jinny knew he was right. Keziah had been ready to die. To upset herself over this was only selfishness, wanting what she couldn't have.

"Will you be back?" Jinny asked.

Again Tam shrugged, not caring. "You'll keep the paints until an old one comes? Don't be showing them to anyone or using them."

"'Course not."

Tam turned, walked back to the bothy and, without looking round, went inside. Jinny waited a long, last minute then she put on Easter's halter and, mounting Shantih, led the pony down the track to Finmory.

"You're coming home," she told Easter. "You'll stay with us for always."

Catching Shantih's freshness, Easter walked freely at Jinny's side, looking eagerly in front of her, and when Bramble whinnied she answered with a clarion blast and broke into a trot, tugging at the halter rope.

"Easy, easy," cried Jinny, as she sat astride Shantih, laughing to see Easter so full of life again.

Ken was waiting for them by the stables. "Keziah?" he asked.

"She's dead," said Jinny.

"She'll know everything now," said Ken, smiling wistfully. "Once we all used to think that the world was flat, go too far and you fell over the edge. Now we all know it's round."

Jinny let Ken's words stay in her mind as they walked down to the field.

"The way we see it isn't the way it is? No edge to fall over?"

"Something like that," agreed Ken.

"Well, anyway," said Jinny, "Easter isn't going to fall over any edge. She's getting better." Reaching the field, she took off Easter's halter and turned her loose.

Bramble came bustling up to her, giving sharp little whickerings of welcome. They stood for a second, nostrils touching, then, standing side by side, began to nibble along each other's necks and withers giving shrill squeals of delight as they did so.

"They know each other," cried Jinny in amazement. At the very least, she had expected Bramble to have a kick or two at Easter. "They do. They must."

"Looks like it," agreed Ken.

Jinny took off Shantih's bridle and the Arab circled the ponies. Tail high, mane bannered, she cast a red-gold ring round them before she began to graze.

Jinny gave a long sigh of relief. Things were back as they should be—Shantih sound, Easter saved; even Keziah's death amongst her own people was the right thing to have happened.

Carrying the paints carefully in her hand, walking backwards so that she could see the ponies and Shantih for as long as possible, Jinny followed Ken back to the house. All manner of things were well.

'JINNY' BOOKS
by Patricia Leitch

When Jinny Manders rescues Shantih, a chestnut Arab,
from a cruel circus, her dreams of owning a horse of her
own seem to come true. But Shantih is wild and unrideable.

This is an exciting and moving series of books about a very
special relationship between a girl and a magnificent horse.

FOR LOVE OF A HORSE
A DEVIL TO RIDE
THE SUMMER RIDERS
NIGHT OF THE RED HORSE
GALLOP TO THE HILLS
HORSE IN A MILLION
THE MAGIC PONY
RIDE LIKE THE WIND
CHESTNUT GOLD
JUMP FOR THE MOON
HORSE OF FIRE

Armada